TALES TO GIVE YOU
Goosebumps

D0170336

Chris Haynes

Look for more Goosebumps books
by R.L. Stine:

TALES TO GIVE YOU
Goosebumps

TEN SPOOKY STORIES

R.L. STINE

AN
APPLE
PAPERBACK

SCHOLASTIC INC.
New York Toronto London Auckland Sydney

A PARACHUTE PRESS BOOK

If you purchased this book without a cover, you should be aware that this book is stolen property. It was reported as "unsold and destroyed" to the publisher, and neither the author nor the publisher has received any payment for this "stripped book."

No part of this publication may be reproduced in whole or in part, or stored in a retrieval system, or transmitted in any form or by any means, electronic, mechanical, photocopying, recording, or otherwise, without written permission of the publisher. For information regarding permission, write to Scholastic Inc., 555 Broadway, New York, NY 10012.

ISBN 0-590-48993-3

Copyright © 1994 by Parachute Press, Inc. All rights reserved. Published by Scholastic Inc. APPLE PAPERBACKS is a registered trademark of Scholastic Inc. GOOSEBUMPS is a trademark of Parachute Press, Inc.

12 11 10 9 8 7 6 5 4 3 2 1   4 5 6 7 8 9/9

Printed in the U.S.A.   40

First Scholastic printing, October 1994

CONTENTS

TALES TO GIVE YOU
Goosebumps

THE HOUSE OF NO RETURN

We were afraid to go too close to the house. So we stayed down at the street, staring up at it. Staring across the bare, sloping front yard.

No grass would grow in that yard. The trees, gnarled and bent, were all dead. Not even weeds sprouted in the dry, cracked dirt.

At the top of the sloping yard, the house seemed to stare back at us. The two upstairs windows gaped like two unblinking black eyes.

The house was wide and solid-looking. Built of bricks. Many years ago, the bricks had been painted white. But now the paint was faded and peeling. Spots of red brick showed through like bloodstains.

The window shutters were cracked. Several had fallen off. The beams of the front porch tilted dangerously. A strong wind could blow the porch over.

No one lived there. The house had been empty for years and years.

No one *could* live there.

The house was haunted. Everyone in town said it was.

Everyone knew the legend of the house: If you spent the night inside it, you would never come out.

That's why we brought kids there. That's why we dared them to go inside.

You couldn't join our Danger Club unless you stayed inside the house — by yourself — for an hour.

Staring up at the house, bathed in a haze of pale moonlight, I shivered. I zipped my windbreaker up to my chin and crossed my arms over my chest.

"How long has he been in there, Robbie?" Nathan asked me.

Lori and I both raised our wrists to check our watches. "Only ten minutes," I told Nathan.

"Fifty minutes to go," Lori said. "Think he'll make it?"

"Doug is pretty brave," I replied thoughtfully, watching the moon disappear behind a cloud. "He might last another five minutes!" I said, grinning.

Lori and Nathan snickered.

The three of us felt safe down here by the street.

Poor Doug probably didn't feel too safe right now. He was shut inside the dark house. Trying to stay there an hour so he could join our club.

I turned and saw a light rolling silently over

the street, coming toward us. A white, ghostly light.

My breath caught in my throat.

It's a car, I realized, as it floated closer. A car with only one headlight. The first car we'd seen on this street all night.

The beam from the headlight washed over my two friends and me, forcing us to shield our eyes. As it passed, we turned back to the house — and heard a shrill scream.

A wail of terror.

"Here he comes!" Nathan cried.

Sure enough, Doug burst out through the front door. He stumbled off the crumbling porch and came tearing across the dead, bare yard.

His hands waved wildly in front of him. His head was tilted back, and his mouth was frozen open in one long, high shriek of fright.

"Doug — what did you see?" I called. "Did you really see a ghost?"

"S-something touched my *face!*" he wailed. He ran right past Nathan, Lori, and me, screaming his head off.

"Probably only a spiderweb," I murmured.

"Robbie — we've got to stop him!" Lori cried.

"Doug! Hey — Doug!" We called his name and chased after him, our sneakers slapping loudly on the pavement.

Waving his arms frantically and screaming, leaning into the wind, Doug kept running.

We couldn't catch him. "He'll run home," I said breathlessly. I stopped and leaned over, pressing my hands against my knees, trying to catch my breath.

Up ahead, we could still hear poor Doug's frightened wail.

"Guess he doesn't join the club," I said, still breathing hard.

"What do we do now?" Nathan asked, glancing back at the house.

"I guess we find another victim," I replied.

Chris Wakely seemed like a perfect victim.

His family had moved to town last summer, and Chris started in my sixth-grade class in September. Chris had pale blue eyes and very short, white-blond hair. He was kind of shy, but he seemed like a really nice guy.

One day after school, I saw Chris walking home and I hurried to catch up with him. It was a windy October day. All around us, red and yellow leaves were falling from the trees. It looked like it was raining leaves.

I said hi to Chris and started telling him about our club. I asked if he'd like to join.

"It's only for brave people," I explained. "In order to join, you have to spend an hour at night inside the house on Willow Hill."

Chris stopped walking and turned to me,

squinting at me with those pale blue eyes. "Isn't that house supposed to be haunted?" he asked.

I laughed. "You don't believe in ghosts — do you?"

He didn't smile. His expression turned serious. The light seemed to fade in his eyes. "I'm not very brave," he said softly.

We started to walk again. Our sneakers crunched on the leaves strewn over the sidewalk. "We'd really like you to join the club," I told him. "You're brave enough to spend one hour in an empty house, aren't you?"

He shrugged and lowered his eyes. "I — I don't think so," he stammered. "I've always been afraid of monsters and things," he admitted. "I believed there was a monster living under my bed until I was eight!"

I laughed. But his expression remained solemn. He wasn't kidding.

"When I go to a scary movie," Chris continued, "I have to duck under the seat when the scary parts come on."

Lori and Nathan came running up to us. "Are you going to do it?" Nathan asked Chris. "Are you going to join the club?"

Chris shoved his hands deep into his jeans pockets. "Did you guys spend an hour in the house?" he asked.

I shook my head. "We don't have to," I told

him. "We started the club, so we don't have to go in the house. We already know we like danger. New members have to prove themselves."

Chris chewed thoughtfully at his lower lip. We turned the corner and kept walking. The house was up the hill, at the end of the block.

We stopped in front of it and stared across the bare front yard. "See? It doesn't look scary at all in the daytime," I said.

Chris swallowed hard. "Needs a paint job," he muttered. "And how come all the trees died?"

"No one to take care of them," Nathan said.

"How about it, Chris?" I urged. "We really need new members."

"Yeah," Lori agreed. "A club isn't much fun with only three kids in it."

Chris had his eyes on the house. He kept his hands jammed into his jeans pockets. I thought I saw him shiver. But it might have been the wind rustling his jacket.

"W-will you come in with me?" he asked.

"No way," I replied, shaking my head.

"We can't," Lori told him. "The idea of the club is to show how brave you are."

"We won't come in," Nathan said. "But we'll wait out front for you."

"Come on, Chris," I urged. "Do it. It'll be fun! It's almost Halloween. Get in the spirit!"

He swallowed a couple of times, staring up at the house. Then he shook his head. "I really don't want to," he murmured in a low voice, so low I could barely hear him. "Guess I'm kind of a scaredy-cat."

I started to plead with him. But I could see he was really embarrassed. So I didn't say any more.

Chris waved good-bye and hurried off toward his house. Lori, Nathan, and I watched him until he disappeared around the corner.

"Now what?" Nathan asked.

We held a club meeting at my house two nights later. It was a pretty boring meeting. None of us could think of another cool kid to join our club. And we couldn't think of anything fun to do.

"Halloween is Saturday," I moaned. "We should be able to think of something scary to do."

"What are you going to dress up as?" Lori asked Nathan.

"Freddy Krueger," Nathan replied. "I already bought the metal fingernails."

"Weren't you Freddy Krueger last year?" I asked him.

"So? I *like* being Freddy Krueger!" Nathan insisted.

"You and every other kid in school," Lori muttered.

Lori planned to dress as a vampire. And I had my monster costume all ready.

"We need more club members," Lori said, sighing. "You can't have a club with just three people."

"Chris would be perfect," I replied. "If only he weren't such a scaredy-cat."

"You know," Nathan started, rubbing his chin thoughtfully, "it would be really good for Chris to get over his fears."

"Huh? What do you mean?" I asked.

"I mean we could help Chris out," Nathan replied, smiling. "We could help him be brave."

I still didn't understand. "Nathan — what are you saying?"

His smile grew wider. "We could *force* him to go into the house."

I called Chris later that night and invited him to go trick-or-treating with us. He said yes. He sounded grateful to have some kids to go around with. He had only been at our school two months, and he hadn't made many friends.

The three of us met at my house on Halloween. Nathan clicked his long metal nails and kept cackling and grinning like Freddy Krueger. I was a very cool monster, with eyeballs on springs popping from my purple head. Lori kept talking in a weird vampire voice.

"Where's Chris?" Nathan asked, looking around. "Is he meeting us here?"

"Yeah. Where is he?" Lori demanded.

We were all a little tense. We were playing a mean trick on Chris. But we knew he'd feel good about things by the end of the night.

8

The doorbell rang, and we all ran to answer it. Chris stood in the porch light, his face an ugly green. He raised both hands to show them to us. They were covered in green, too.

"What are *you* supposed to be — a pea pod?" I joked.

Chris looked hurt. "No. I'm a corpse."

"Very scary," I said. I handed out trick-or-treat bags. "Let's get going." I led the way down the driveway and up the street.

We stopped at several houses and collected candy. It was a cool, windy night with a tiny sliver of a moon. Gusts of wind kept fluttering our costumes and making our trick-or-treat bags fly up.

We were approaching the house on Willow Hill. I had a heavy feeling in my stomach. My hands suddenly felt ice cold.

I hope Chris can stay in the house for a whole hour, I thought. He's such a nice guy. I'd really like him to be in the club.

Such a nice guy. And we were about to do such a mean thing to him.

But he'll quickly get over it, I told myself. And he'll be glad we made him test his bravery.

The eerie house came into view. I saw Chris glance at it, then quickly turn to cross the street. He didn't want to go near it. Especially on Halloween night.

But Nathan and I grabbed him by the arms.

9

Chris cried out in surprise. "Hey — let go! What are you guys doing?"

Chris struggled to pull free. But Nathan and I were much bigger than him, and stronger.

Lori led the way over the bare, dirt yard, up the sloping hill to the dark, silent house. Chris tried to swing both arms, tried desperately to break free. But Nathan and I dragged him onto the tilting porch, up to the front door.

"No! Please!" Chris pleaded. "Please — don't do this! Don't!"

I turned to him. Even under the green makeup, I could see the terror on his face. The poor guy was totally freaked!

"Chris, you'll be okay," I said softly, soothingly. "Go inside. It'll be fun. We'll wait for you. I promise."

"You'll be proud of yourself," Lori told him, helping to push him up to the door. "And then you'll be in our club."

Lori started to push open the heavy door. Nathan and I moved to shove Chris inside. But to my surprise, he reached out and grabbed my arm.

"Come in with me — please!" he begged, his eyes wide with fright. "Please! I'm too scared! I'm just too scared!" He held on tightly to my arm. "Let's all go in together — okay?"

I glanced at Lori and Nathan. "No way," I replied. "You've got to prove your bravery, Chris. See you in an hour."

We gave him a hard shove inside the house. Then we slammed the heavy door behind him.

"He seems so . . . scared," Lori said, her voice muffled by the vampire fangs.

"He'll be okay," I said. "Let's wait for him down by the street."

We took our places at the bottom of the driveway, and waited.

And waited.

We checked our watches after ten minutes. After twenty minutes. After half an hour.

"Chris is doing great!" I whispered, my eyes on the dark windows of the house. "I didn't think he'd last *two* minutes."

"He's a lot braver than I thought," Nathan said from behind his Freddy Krueger mask.

We huddled close together, staring up at the house as the wind shook the trees all around us. Heavy clouds rolled over the moon, covering us in darkness.

We waited ten minutes more. Then ten minutes more.

"He's going to do it," I said, checking my watch again. "He's going to stay in there for a whole hour."

"Let's really give him a big cheer when he comes out," Lori suggested.

As the hour ended, we counted off the last thirty seconds out loud, one by one. Then we took a few steps up the driveway, eager to congratulate

Chris and welcome him to the Danger Club.

But the front door didn't open. The house remained dark and silent.

Ten more minutes passed.

"I think he's showing off," I said.

No one laughed. We kept our eyes raised to the house.

Ten more minutes. Then ten more.

"Where *is* he?" I cried shrilly.

"Something is wrong," Lori said, taking the plastic vampire fangs out of her mouth. "Something is wrong, Robbie."

"Chris should be out of there by now," Nathan agreed in a trembling voice.

I felt a chill run down my back. All of my muscles were tightening in dread. I knew my friends were right. Something bad had happened inside that house. Something very bad.

"We have to go in there," Lori urged. "We have to find Chris. We have to get him out."

All three of us exchanged frightened glances. We didn't want to walk up that driveway. We didn't want to go inside that dark house.

But we didn't have a choice.

"Maybe we should wait a few more minutes," I suggested, trying to stop my legs from shaking. "Maybe he doesn't have a watch. Maybe he's — "

"Come on, Robbie." Lori gave me a hard tug. "Chris isn't coming out. We have to go get him."

The wind swirled around us, fluttering our costumes as we made our way up to the front door. I started to open the door, but my hand was so sweaty, the doorknob slid under my grasp.

Finally, Nathan and I pushed open the heavy door. The rusty hinges creaked as we opened the door and peered into the solid blackness.

"Chris?" I called. "Chris — you can come out now!" My voice sounded tiny and hollow.

No reply.

"Chris? Chris? Where are you?" All three of us began calling him.

The floor groaned and creaked beneath us as we took a few steps into the living room. The wind rattled the old windowpanes.

"Chris — can you hear us? Chris?"

No reply.

A loud crash made all three of us cry out.

The front door had slammed behind us.

"J-just the wind, guys," I choked out.

It was much darker with the door closed. But it didn't stay dark for long. Pale light flickered at the top of the stairs. It looked at first like dozens of fireflies clustered together.

I gasped as the light flared brighter. And floated down the stairs, like a shimmering cloud.

"Let's get out!" I cried.

Too late.

The shimmering cloud spread around us. And inside it I saw two frightening figures — a ghostly

13

man and woman, hazy and transparent except for their red, glowing eyes.

Their terrifying eyes sparkled like fiery coals as they circled us, floating silently.

I can see right through both of them! I realized. This house really is haunted.

"Wh-where's Chris?" I managed to blurt out.

The man's voice was a dry whisper, the sound of wind through dead leaves. "Your friend? He went out the back door," the ghost replied. "About an hour ago."

"We didn't want to let him go," the woman whispered, her red eyes glowing brighter. "But he made a bargain with us." She snickered, a dry, dead laugh. "He promised that if we let him go, three kids would come in to take his place."

"And here you are," said the ghostly man, flashing an ugly, toothless smile. "Here you are."

"Don't look so frightened, kids," the woman rasped, floating closer. "You might as well make yourselves at home. You're all going to be here — *forever!*"

TEACHER'S PET

Do you like snakes?

If you're in Mr. Blankenship's class, you *have* to like snakes — or you're in *major* trouble!

Let me start at the beginning, on the first day of school last September. Benjy, my best friend, was shouting to me from my front porch. "Becca, move it! We'll be late!"

I grabbed my black denim jacket and tucked my ponytail under my New York Yankees baseball cap. I hurried, even though I knew Benjy would never leave without me.

Benjy and I had walked to school together every day since kindergarten. Some people think it's weird that a girl and a guy are best friends. But Benjy and I don't care. We've always liked to do the same sort of stuff — like play basketball and baseball, and cook. (Benjy would kill me if he knew I told anyone about that!)

Benjy and I were starting sixth grade. At our

school, sixth-graders get to do great stuff — like go on a camp-out for a whole week!

We were supposed to have Ms. Wenger this year, the coolest teacher in the whole school. Ms. Wenger is the kind of teacher who takes the whole class in-line skating so that when someone falls down, she can talk to us about gravity!

Benjy and I figured this would be just about the best school year ever.

So you can imagine our surprise when we walked into our classroom and saw the teacher writing his name on the board. The teacher wasn't Ms. Wenger. It was a man named Mr. Blankenship.

Benjy and I both groaned in disappointment. Mr. Blankenship was a strange-looking dude. He was really, really tall and really, really skinny. And he was almost completely bald.

His clothes were pretty bad, too. Especially the weird turtleneck sweater he was wearing with the beige, brown, and black diamonds all over it.

He greeted Benjy and me at the door and asked our names.

"I'm Becca Thompson," I said.

"Benjy Connor," Benjy said.

"I'm just getting things together right now. Why don't you two join the others and take a tour around the room?" Mr. Blankenship suggested.

The room looked pretty dull — not cool the way Ms. Wenger would have done it. Mr. Blankenship had set up the typical stuff — reading corner, computer corner, and a corny "Welcome Back" bulletin board.

The only unusual things were the five or six glass tanks placed around the classroom. I walked over to one of the tanks and pressed my nose up against the glass. Not much to see — some rocks, a pile of dried grass, a stick, and . . .

"Aaagh!" I uttered a shriek.

Then I just stood there, pointing at the long, skinny, hissing creature. I hate snakes. I can't help it. I just hate them!

I hate those tiny, black eyes that sort of stare right through you. That's what scares me the most — those eyes.

I wanted to turn away from the snake's angry glare, but I couldn't. I seemed to be paralyzed. Frozen stiff. And my heart was pounding so hard, I thought it was going to pop out of my chest!

It was Benjy who broke the snake's spell over me. He came over and shoved me out of the way to get a better view. "Oh. A snake," he said calmly. But I knew that Benjy is just as afraid of snakes as I am.

"I see you've met one of my little pals," Mr. Blankenship said to us, smiling. "We're going to study snakes this year. Fascinating creatures. Fascinating."

Leaning over the cage, Mr. Blankenship turned to me. "Did you know that snakes can live for

17

months without food? Of course, they'd much rather swallow a tasty little mouse instead. Watch."

He reached into a smaller cage hidden behind a bookshelf and grabbed a small white mouse by the tail. The mouse tried to wriggle free, but Mr. Blankenship held tight to its slender pink tail.

He dangled the thrashing, wriggling mouse over the snake's tank for a few seconds. Then he dropped it right next to the snake.

I didn't want to watch. But I couldn't help myself.

The snake snapped open its jaws, and swallowed the little white mouse — whole! I let out a groan as I watched the pink tail slide past the snake's teeth like a spaghetti noodle.

I felt really sick to my stomach. But there was no way I was giving Mr. Blankenship the satisfaction of knowing he had totally grossed me out.

"Who's next?" Mr. Blankenship asked, rubbing his long, slender hands together. "Who's hungry?"

That's when I realized that *all* of the glass cages in the room were filled with Mr. Blankenship's slimy, slithering, hissing little "pals."

Benjy and I tried to like Mr. Blankenship's class. But it wasn't easy. For one thing, he kept adding more and more snakes. Soon, one entire wall was filled with glass tanks.

The snakes slithered silently, their black eyes

following Mr. Blankenship. "There are more snakes than kids in here!" I whispered to Benjy one day.

It seemed as if Mr. Blankenship could talk about nothing else! In science, we studied about the hatching of snake eggs. For history, we read stories about ancient beliefs in serpents. For geometry, we made chalk drawings of snakeskin patterns.

One enormous glass cage behind Mr. Blankenship's desk stood empty. Benjy and I wondered what he planned to put in there. "A giant python!" Benjy guessed.

I shuddered. I didn't want to think about it.

Every time I peered into a glass cage and saw a snake staring back at me, I panicked. I knew the snakes hated being cooped up in those tanks. Something in their eyes told me that if they ever got out, they would go for the first human they saw.

I hoped it wasn't me!

One night I was lying in bed, trying to get to sleep. Pale moonlight washed over my room from the open window. I saw a shadow move against the wall.

Uttering a frightened gasp, I clicked on my bed-table lamp.

And saw a snake slithering out of my backpack on the floor.

How had it escaped from its tank? How had it crept into my backpack?

Frozen in terror, I watched it slither over my shag rug, making its way to my bed.

I screamed and forced myself to sit up. I tried to scramble away. But I felt something warm and dry curl around my arm.

"Uh-uh-uh-uh — !" I was making this weird gasping sound. I felt something like a rope tightening around my ankle. Another snake slithered over my pillow. Two more snakes crawled over my pajama legs.

"Hellllp!" My frantic plea escaped my lips in a hushed whisper.

The snakes tightened themselves around me, curling around my waist, my arms, my legs. One of them slithered through my hair.

I started to shudder and shake. I shook so hard, I woke myself up.

What a horrible nightmare!

Mr. Blankenship and his room full of snakes were ruining my life. But what could I do?

The next day I tried to switch my seat to one far away from the snake tanks. But the tanks were everywhere, on the shelves, on the tables, stacked along the window ledges. Every day there seemed to be more of them.

I tried hard not to think about the snakes around the room. I tried to concentrate on our geography lesson — the snakes of New Mexico.

But just as Mr. Blankenship began to discuss the heat of the desert, I heard a *thud*. Then Melissa Potter let out a shrill scream.

"I'm sorry!" she cried. "I bumped a cage. I let out one of the mice!"

"Where? Where did it go?" Mr. Blankenship cried excitedly.

"There it goes!" Benjy cried, pointing. The little white mouse scampered across the floor. Kids screamed and laughed.

But Mr. Blankenship had a serious, angry expression on his face. "Grab it! Grab it — quick!" he shouted.

"It's over there!" shouted Carl Jansen, pointing to the window in the corner. Mr. Blankenship always left that window open so his snake pals could get fresh air.

Mr. Blankenship dived across the room. The mouse scuttled onto the window ledge. Mr. Blankenship grabbed for the tail. Missed. The mouse vanished out the window.

Our teacher turned beet-red. Even the top of his bald head was red. "Now look what you've done!" he screamed at Melissa. "You let a perfectly good snake dinner get away!

"You will all have to be taught to be more careful," Mr. Blankenship bellowed. "Perhaps an extra homework assignment will help you remember. I want three pages on the feeding habits of the eastern diamondback rattler. And I want it tomorrow!"

"What is his problem?" I whispered to Benjy.

"Becca!" Mr. Blankenship shouted. "I heard that! *You* will write a *ten*-page essay!"

"But — but — !" I sputtered.

"And you will clean the snake cages for the next two weeks!" Mr. Blankenship added.

I clamped my hand over my mouth to keep myself from getting in even worse trouble. But I was so angry, I could have let *all* the mice out of their cages!

Which gave me a great idea. "Benjy," I whispered when Mr. Blankenship had turned away. "After school. My house. Get ready for Operation Mouse Rescue."

Later, after school, Benjy and I worked out all of the details. Operation Mouse Rescue would take place on Thursday night, after our parents went to play bridge.

The plan was simple. Simple, but excellent. Benjy and I were going to sneak into school and set all of the white mice free. We could just picture Mr. Blankenship's face when he arrived Friday morning and found the mice scampering all over the room.

Thursday seemed to stretch on forever. I barely heard a word Mr. Blankenship said. I was too busy watching the clock, waiting for the bell to ring.

I know I ate dinner with my family — but don't ask me what we had. All I could think about was Operation Mouse Rescue.

Finally, my parents said good-bye, left all the right phone numbers, and drove off to their bridge tournament. It didn't take long before Benjy gave me our secret signal — a single ring of the telephone.

My heart pounding, I pulled on my black jeans and dark jacket and raced up the block to Benjy's house. He was waiting for me at the bottom of the driveway.

"What took you so long?" he demanded. "You're not wimping out — are you?"

"No way!" I replied, although I suddenly felt as if *I* had white mice fluttering around in my stomach. "Let's go."

Half walking, half jogging, we made our way to school. It was a cool, breezy night. The trees shivered, shedding fat brown leaves. Shadows twisted and bent over our path as we crept up to the dark school building.

"Around the back," I whispered.

The school seemed so much larger, so much scarier at night, bathed in total blackness.

We found our classroom. Benjy clicked on his flashlight.

"No — turn it off!" I instructed. "Someone may see us."

He obediently clicked off the light. We spotted

the open window, the window in the corner that Mr. Blankenship always leaves open.

My hands felt cold and wet as I grabbed the stone window ledge and pulled myself up. Inside the room, I turned and helped pull Benjy in.

"It — it's so dark," he whispered, huddling close to me. "Can't we turn on the flashlights?"

"Okay," I whispered back. "But keep the light down on the floor."

Our circles of yellow light swept over the floor. Slowly, we made our way to the table that held the mice cages. The floorboards creaked under our sneakers.

I glanced nervously around the room. Tiny lights flickered in the blackness. It took me a long moment to realize they weren't lights. They were glowing snake eyes.

"They — they're all watching us," I whispered to Benjy. "The snakes — they're — "

So many glowing eyes. So many snakes! All around us. Staring. Staring.

I forgot to watch where I was going. I stumbled over a chair.

"Ow!" I cried out. I tried to catch my balance, but fell against a table.

A glass tank toppled to the floor with a shattering *crash*. I glanced down in time to see two snakes slither onto the floor. They uncurled in the trembling light of my flashlight. Then moved quickly toward my legs.

"Benjy — help!" I thrashed out my arms. I turned to run. And knocked over another snake cage.

A long black snake rolled silently onto the floor, arched itself up, opened its jaws, and shot its head toward me.

"Run!" I shrieked. "Benjy — the snakes are out!"

"How — ?" Benjy started.

I jumped as a snake slithered between my feet.

We turned to run — but stopped as our lights played over the enormous, empty glass case.

Which wasn't empty anymore.

A giant gray-and-black cobra glared into the shaking lights. The cobra arched its head up, opened its jaws, and hissed at us, its red eyes gleaming excitedly.

When did that snake get in there? I asked myself. The cage was empty this afternoon!

"R-run!" I stammered, grabbing Benjy's shoulder.

But neither of us could move. We stood staring in frozen horror as the enormous cobra rose up. Lifted itself up. Out of the cage.

It stood over us, at least six feet tall. Its eyes glowing. Its thick tongue flicking across its open jaws.

And as it rose up, its skin shifted and stretched. Its head tilted up. Its body grew wide. Grew arms. Legs.

And we recognized him. We saw him. We knew him.

We knew we were staring at Mr. Blankenship. The snake was Mr. Blankenship!

"Noooooooo!" Did that terrified howl escape *my* throat? Or was Benjy howling like some unearthly creature?

I only knew that we turned and ran. Dived out through the open window. Into the dark night. And kept running. Running till we were safe at home. Safe. Safe from snakes. Safe from the biggest snake — Mr. Blankenship.

But safe for how long? Safe till we had to return to school the next morning?

Trembling with fright, Benjy and I hesitated at the classroom door on Friday morning. What would Mr. Blankenship do to us now that we knew his horrible secret? What would he say?

He smiled as Benjy and I entered, and didn't say a word. The day went by like any other day. He didn't say a word about what had happened the night before.

Until the final bell rang that afternoon. He dismissed the rest of the class, then turned to Benjy and me. "I want you two to stay," he said sternly. He moved quickly to block the doorway.

We were alone with him now. He closed the door and moved toward us, rubbing his slender hands together, his dark eyes glowing excitedly.

*　　　*　　　*

Mr. Blankenship isn't such a bad guy. He made us a deal. He said he wouldn't tell anyone we broke into the school. And he promised not to harm us as long as we didn't tell anyone his secret.

Of course Benjy and I quickly agreed.

There's just one part of the deal that I hate.

We have to bring in white mice and feed him every afternoon.

I really hate the way the mice wriggle and squirm as I hold them up by their pink tails.

But what choice do I have?

A deal's a deal.

"Here you go, Mr. Blankenship. Open wide."

STRAINED PEAS

My life changed forever the day Mom brought the new baby home from the hospital. My little sister is no ordinary baby.

If only she were.

I sat on the front steps with Mrs. Morgan, waiting for Mom and Dad to bring the baby home. Mrs. Morgan had stayed with me and Dad while Mom was in the hospital.

I thought about the new baby. Hannah. A little sister.

Yuck.

I sighed and tapped a stick against the brick steps.

"Stop fidgeting, Nicholas," Mrs. Morgan scolded. "Why don't you read your comic book until your parents get home?"

I opened my *Iron Man* comic book and picked up where I'd left off. Iron Man has cornered a bad guy disguised as a kindly doctor. "Unmask yourself!" says Iron Man.

Iron Man rips the mask off the doctor's head, revealing the hideous face of a mad scientist. Iron Man gasps. "The Mark of Evil!" he cries. "Dr. Destro!"

Iron Man has never seen Dr. Destro before, but he recognizes the bad guy by the birthmark on his face — the Mark of Evil.

I heard a car coming and glanced up. Dad's dark green Volvo chugged down the street and pulled into our driveway. Mom sat in the passenger seat, waving to me and smiling brightly.

Mrs. Morgan gave me a little shove. "Go on," she said. "Go meet your new sister!"

Ugh, I thought. I *was* glad to see Mom, though. I dragged myself over to the car.

Dad opened the car door. Mom stepped out, carrying a little bundle in her arms. She bent down and said, "Look, Nicholas. Isn't she adorable?"

I looked at the crumpled red face in my mother's arms. A thin fuzz of dark hair covered her head. She had blue eyes and tiny, wet red lips. No teeth. She waved a wrinkled fist in the air, then stuffed it into her mouth.

I didn't think she was so adorable. I thought she was kind of ugly.

But then I nearly choked. On Hannah's cheek was a tiny, brown, heart-shaped birthmark.

I pointed to the birthmark and gasped, "The Mark of Evil! Just like Dr. Destro!"

"Cut it out, Nicholas," Dad said sternly. "This is no time for your crazy comic book talk."

He turned his back on me to gawk at Hannah.

"She's perfect," Dad said, giving Mom's shoulders a squeeze.

How could he be so stupid? I picked up my comic book and pointed to the mark on Dr. Destro's face.

"Look!" I cried. "Hannah has a birthmark like Dr. Destro's! It's a sign of evil!"

Mom smiled vaguely at me. "Don't be silly," she said. She carried the baby inside, and the rest of us followed her.

Soon Grandma and Grandpa came over, and Aunt Julie and Uncle Hal. They oohed and ahhed every time Hannah burped, or hiccupped, or cooed. It was disgusting.

"Look at that — she blew a bubble!"

"She's a genius!"

"Dori, darling, let me hold her for a few minutes," Grandma begged Mom.

But Mom said, "Let Nicholas hold her. He's her big brother, after all."

"No," I said, backing away. "That's okay."

"Oh, come on, Nick. You'll like it." Mom smiled and put Hannah in my arms. She showed me how to hold her. Hannah burped. Everyone laughed.

As I held her, I thought, she's sort of cute, I guess. Maybe I got a little carried away with that Mark of Evil stuff. After all, comic books don't come true. And Hannah's just a baby.

31

But like I said, she was no ordinary baby.

I swear I saw something glint in her dark blue eyes.

That little heart-shaped birthmark on her cheek seemed to darken.

Then Hannah opened her mouth wide — and threw up all over me.

"Ugh!" I cried. I was covered with milky white glop.

Mom quickly took the baby.

Hannah started crying. "Poor little Hannah," Mom said.

Poor little Hannah! *I* was the one she threw up on!

And she did it on purpose. I knew she did.

That night, the howling began.

A horrible sound woke me up. A loud, screeching wail.

I sat up in bed, shaking. My eardrums rattled in my ears.

What was that noise?

I got out of bed to see what was going on. Mom was walking Hannah up and down the hallway, patting and shushing her. But Hannah didn't stop screaming. She sounded like some kind of wild animal in pain.

"Mom — what's wrong with her?" I asked.

"Nothing," Mom replied. "It's just a normal baby sound. Go back to sleep."

I didn't get any sleep. Hannah never stopped crying.

That's no normal baby sound, I thought. No one can tell me that terrifying screech is normal.

Hannah's wailing continued, night after night. Each night was worse than the last. Wild screams that even the neighbors could hear. Monstrous screams. When Hannah started crying, the neighborhood dogs threw their heads back and howled along with her.

I could swear I saw her birthmark grow, just a little.

A few months passed. Hannah learned to crawl early. Mom and Dad thought that meant she was smart. I knew better.

She had a mission. She wanted to be an only child.

She wanted to get rid of me.

The crying didn't get rid of me. The puking didn't get rid of me.

But Hannah had other tricks up her little terry-cloth sleeve.

One morning before school I found Hannah in my room, chewing on something. She held a bit of paper in her hand. When she saw me coming, she tried to stuff it into her mouth. I snatched it away from her.

"Oh, no!" I cried. "My math homework!"

Or what was left of it. Mostly just my name and the date. Covered with drool.

Hannah had eaten my homework.

She swallowed and smiled that evil smile.

Ha-ha, her smile seemed to say. Gotcha.

"Mom!" I called. "Hannah ate my homework!"

Mom swooped in and picked up Hannah. "She *what*? Is she all right?"

"Mom! What about my homework?"

Mom frowned at me as if she just realized what I was telling her.

"Nicholas, you didn't do your homework, did you? And now you're trying to blame it on Hannah!"

"Mom, I'm telling the truth! Give Hannah an X ray. You'll see my homework in her stomach!"

Mom shook her head. "Nicholas, what's wrong with you lately?"

Later that day, when my teacher asked me where my math homework was, I told her my baby sister had eaten it.

She kept me after school.

That's what I got for telling the truth.

"Nicholas! Get in here! I want to talk to you!" Dad called.

I was playing in the backyard when his voice boomed at me from an upstairs window.

I found Dad in my parents' bedroom. At least I *thought* it was their room. It was where their room was supposed to be. Only it didn't look much like their room anymore.

Normally, my parents' room was white. I mean WHITE. White rugs, white walls, white curtains, white bedspread. I wasn't allowed to play in there, or eat, or do anything. They were always worried about all that white stuff.

The room wasn't white anymore. It was multi-colored. Paint splashed everywhere.

"Nicholas," Dad said. "You are in big trouble. Huge trouble."

Little jars of paint from my paint set littered the floor. Red, blue, green, yellow, and black paints were splashed all over the white rug, the white curtains, the white bedspread, the white walls. And in the middle of it all, splattered with blood-red paint, Hannah sat laughing her evil laugh.

"You have one minute to give me an explanation for this, Nicholas," Dad said. "Go."

"I didn't do it," I said. "Hannah did it."

Dad laughed sarcastically. "Hannah did it? Hannah took your paint set, brought it all the way to our room, opened the jars, and splattered paint all over everything?"

"Yes," I said.

"Nicholas, go to your room."

"But, Dad — I didn't do anything wrong!"

"Oh, no? Go to your room and think about it until you can see what you did wrong."

"Dad — Hannah did it! She did it on purpose —

to get me in trouble! You're playing right into her hands!"

Dad gave me his stony glare. He pointed to my room.

I went. There's no fighting Dad's stony glare.

She's a monster, I thought. She's really a monster.

But she won't get away with this. I'll find a way to convince them, somehow. I'm not leaving this family. *She* is.

The next day, when I came home from school, I heard terrible screams from the kitchen.

I ran in. Hannah sat in her high chair, screaming with laughter. My mother stood beside her. Mom, Hannah, the floor, the walls — all covered with green slime.

Green slime oozed out of the corner of Hannah's mouth.

Hannah had spewed green slime everywhere.

"She's a monster!" I shouted. "This is proof!"

Mom ignored me. "Hannah, you naughty girl!" she said. "Strained peas all over the kitchen!"

Hannah banged her spoon on her high-chair tray. More green stuff splattered on the wall.

All right. It wasn't exactly green slime. But it was close enough. Strained peas. They're green, and they're slimy.

Mom said, "Nicholas, get a sponge and help me clean this up."

"Why do I have to clean it? *She* made the mess!"

"Nicholas, I'm tired. Just help me out, please."

I stared at Hannah's pea-covered face. Something was different. Her eyes. Her eyes — were brown!

"Mom!" I cried. "Hannah's eyes changed colors! I told you she had evil powers!"

Mom just laughed. "Most babies are born with blue eyes," she explained. "Sometimes their eyes change after a few — "

"Mom, that's impossible! People's eyes don't change color!"

"Yes, they do, Nicholas. Some babies — "

I grabbed her by the arms and tried to shake some sense into her. "Mom — you're losing it. Hannah's brainwashing you! She's trying to get rid of me! We've got to send her back — before it's too late!"

"Nicholas, that's enough! You've been jealous of Hannah from the beginning. It's time for you to get over all of this and start acting a little more mature!"

I felt like tearing my hair out. Why wouldn't my parents believe me? How could I get them to see what Hannah was doing?

Mom started cleaning the strained peas from Hannah's face. The birthmark seemed to glow like a tiny spark.

The worst was still to come.

I was sitting in the den, watching TV. Minding my own business. Then I heard a creeping sound.

Creep, creep, creep. The sound of little knees scraping against the rug.

Oh, no, I thought. Here she comes.

I turned around to look. Hannah was crawling toward me — clutching a pair of scissors in her tiny fist!

She crawled closer, closer, that evil gleam in her eye, the birthmark pulsing on her face.

She was going to stab me!

"NO!" I yelled. I backed away. She kept crawling toward me, the scissors gleaming.

This is it, I thought. My baby sister is going to kill me.

"Nicholas!" My mom stood in the doorway. Then she ran to Hannah and snatched the scissors away from her.

"Thanks, Mom. You saved my life!" I cried.

"How could you *do* this?" Mom said. "How could you let Hannah carry around such a sharp object! She could have been seriously hurt!"

"*She* could have been hurt! Mom, she was going to kill me!"

"Nicholas, this is ridiculous."

"Mom, she's trying to get rid of me! She wants to be an only child!"

"I think that's what *you* want, Nicholas," Mom said. "I think we need to have a long, long talk."

"I'm not making this up, Mom! Why won't you believe me? You always trusted me before — until Hannah came along!"

38

The phone rang. Mom picked up Hannah and stormed off to the kitchen to answer it.

A few minutes later, I heard Mom cry out, "Oh, no! No! I don't believe it!"

I hurried to the kitchen to see what was wrong.

Mom was crying. She said, "All right, Dr. Davis. We'll be there this afternoon."

She hung up the phone and cried some more. She gripped the wall as if she thought she'd faint. Then she stopped crying and stared at Hannah with a new, weird look on her face. A look of horror.

At last, I thought. She believes me!

The doctor must have called to warn us that Hannah is a monster!

"That was the hospital," Mom said in a slow, hoarse voice. "They said . . . they said — "

"That Hannah's a monster!" I finished for her.

Mom turned sharply to me. "Nicholas, stop it!" She scooped Hannah up and hugged her tightly, crying.

"I can't believe it," she said. "I love her so much. But she's not really our baby."

"What?" I was afraid I hadn't heard her right. It seemed too good to be true. Had Mom just said Hannah was not really our baby?

"Our real baby and Hannah were switched at birth," Mom said through her tears. "Hannah is someone else's child."

Hannah wasn't my sister at all. Her real parents

39

were probably monsters, too. It explained everything.

"Yippee!" I shouted. I was free! Free from Hannah's evil! Everything would be okay now. We'd get my *real* baby sister, and she'd be cute and normal like other babies. She wouldn't try to get rid of me. She wouldn't be a monster.

Mom started crying harder than ever. She carried Hannah upstairs to her room and shut the door.

I felt a little bit sorry. Mom was really upset. I knew Dad would be, too.

But they'll be happier when we get our real baby, I thought. And so will I.

Dad came home from work early. We bundled Hannah up and took her to the hospital. A nurse introduced us to a woman who held a baby Hannah's age. Hannah's real mother. She had a tiny heart-shaped birthmark on her cheek, just like Hannah's.

Monster Mom, I thought, even though she didn't look like a monster at all.

The nurse gave my mother the new baby. It seemed weird to call the new baby Hannah, so Mom decided to name her Grace.

When we got home, the first thing I did was check Gracie for birthmarks. She was clean. No birthmarks anywhere.

She was a sweet baby, blond, blue-eyed, smiling, and rosy-cheeked. She looked like an angel. She smiled and cooed at me.

I watched Gracie carefully the first day. Just to be sure.

She didn't cry like an animal. She didn't spew peas or try to stab me. She did nothing but gurgle and coo.

By the end of the day, I thought, she's normal! She's not a monster. She's not out to get me. She's even cute!

Everything is going to be okay now.

Mom put Gracie to bed. I sneaked into her room to play with her for a few minutes.

I tickled her. She giggled. I tickled her again. This time she didn't giggle so much. So I tickled her one more time.

She opened her mouth and croaked, "If you tickle me again, kid, I'll rip your arm off!"

Her eyes bulged as she uttered a deep growl.

"Aaaauuugh!" I wailed. "A monster!"

I ran from the room, screaming my head off. And as I was leaving, I heard the baby cackle, "I'll get rid of you, creep. Just wait till I can walk!"

STRANGERS IN
THE WOODS

"This ruins everything, Lucy," wailed Jessica when I called her to deliver the bad news. "I can't believe you're getting shipped off to . . . what's the name of that town, anyway?"

"Fairview," I said, with a long, very sad sigh. I twisted the phone cord around and around my finger. "I could just *cry*."

I'm not usually so depressed. Actually, Jessica says I'm annoyingly happy most of the time.

But finding out that I'd be spending six weeks this summer with Great-Aunt Abigail in her boring farm town was enough to put me in a bad mood forever. I mean, there's *nothing* in Fairview but tractors and cows and cornfields.

I hoped that something exciting had happened to Fairview since my last visit to Great-Aunt Abigail's two summers before. But when Dad pulled the car into town, the place looked even duller and drabber than I remembered. One grocery, a hardware store, a gas station, and a tiny library.

43

We bumped our way down Great-Aunt Abigail's long dirt road and pulled up in front of 25 Butterfly Lane, her small, redbrick house. I climbed out of the car and looked around. Fields and forests as far as I could see.

Great-Aunt Abigail came running out, dressed in her usual flowered housedress and sneakers. She looked a little different than I remembered, a little older, a little more wrinkled, a little skinnier.

We all greeted one another. Then Mom and Dad followed Great-Aunt Abigail into the house to have tea.

I started to let my dog Muttster out of the car so that he could explore the yard. But the big brown mutt pulled back, his tail between his legs.

"Muttster — what's your problem?" I asked. He acted like a big scaredy-cat, whimpering and huddling in the backseat.

When I finally coaxed him out with a doggie pretzel, he started barking really loud, and running around and around in circles.

The thing you have to know about Muttster is that he *never* barks. He's really well-behaved. That's why he was being allowed to stay in Fairview with me while Mom and Dad went off on their big trip to Asia.

I should have known that something was terribly wrong as soon as Muttster started barking.

But I didn't guess. I just figured the big dog was excited.

Then when Great-Aunt Abigail came outside to see what all the fuss was about, Muttster really went crazy — growling and snapping like a mean old junkyard hound.

"Oh, dear, Lucy," she said nervously. "Why is he doing that? Maybe you should put him in the yard."

I didn't want to tie him up. But Muttster was just going ballistic! So I tied him to a huge oak tree and ran back to the porch to say good-bye to my parents.

"Honey, I'll miss you," Mom said. "You won't be able to call us because we'll be moving around so much. But we'll call when we can and send lots of postcards."

After a lot of hugs and kisses, my parents were off on their trip. I waved sadly, until their car disappeared down the long driveway.

What a boring summer this is going to be, I thought glumly.

I had no idea how *wrong* I was.

Great-Aunt Abigail did her best to cheer me up. "I have a surprise for you, dear," she said. "Your favorite cookies."

Cookies? I'd almost forgotten that Great-Aunt Abigail made the best peanut-butter fudgies in the world.

I took a cookie off the tray she offered. Still warm and soft from the oven. I bit into it eagerly. It was chewy and fudgey and peanut buttery — but something was wrong. Something didn't taste right.

Was it too salty? Were the ingredients different?

How weird, I thought. Great-Aunt Abigail's cookies are always perfect.

I could see her watching me eagerly, so I finished the cookie and pretended to love it. Then I jammed a few cookies in my pocket and threw on my denim jacket. "I'm taking Muttster for a walk," I called out. "Just to relax him."

"Have fun, dear," she said. "But stay out of the woods, okay?"

That's weird, I thought. She never warned me away from the woods during my other visits.

Muttster and I had a nice walk in the sloping, green fields. At times, the dog seemed as calm and playful as always. But then he would start barking excitedly again — for no reason at all.

I couldn't get to sleep that night. Maybe it was because Muttster had to spend the night outside as punishment for his constant barking. At home, he *always* slept at the foot of my bed.

I tried reading a book, but that only made me feel more awake. So I gazed out the window and counted the stars.

And that's when I saw the frightening lights.

In the purple night sky. Six lights, forming a circle.

At first, I thought they were super-bright stars because they were up in the sky. But then I realized they were moving, lowering slowly to the ground.

As I stared with my mouth hanging open in amazement, the lights hovered over the woods on the other side of Great-Aunt Abigail's cornfield. I felt their light washing over me — brightening my whole room, bright as daylight.

Then, slowly, the circle of lights lowered into the woods. And it became dark again.

A cold shudder shook my body. What had I just seen?

I crept down the hall to Great-Aunt Abigail's room and called softly outside her closed door. But she has always been a sound sleeper. She didn't wake up.

Back in my room, I could hear Muttster down in the yard, barking furiously. I shut the window tight. How would I ever get to sleep?

"Do you know what those lights are out in the woods?" I asked Great-Aunt Abigail as I sat down to breakfast.

She narrowed her eyes at me. I thought I saw her cheeks go pink. "Lights? What lights, dear? How do you want your eggs?"

"Scrambled, please. There were about six lights, all in a circle. They were so weird."

"Don't worry, dear. I'm sure it's just reflections or something. Have you fed Muttster?"

Why is she so eager to change the subject? I wondered. Why does she seem so nervous?

Her scrambled eggs tasted different, too. Not as fluffy and fresh-tasting as in the past.

After I ate, I took Muttster his breakfast, a bowl of dry dog food. Then I sat on the lawn, talking to the dog, and staring at the woods — hoping to see something, *anything*, that might explain those lights.

Thinking about those lights made me feel strange. You know how your stomach feels after you've eaten five slices of pizza? That was it, only more nervous and fluttery.

My stomach felt even funnier after Great-Aunt Abigail and I took a drive to the hardware store. Did I say "drive"? It was more like a roller coaster ride!

To my shock, my usually careful great-aunt drove like a maniac! We almost clipped the mailbox on the way out of the driveway. Then she kept weaving from lane to lane and whizzing right through stop signs. I held on to the dashboard, too terrified to scream.

I got my voice back when we finally pulled over on Main Street. "Aunt Abigail!" I cried breathlessly. "Is there something wrong with the car? Why are you driving like this?"

"Like what?" she replied innocently.

The only thing more frightening than the drive to town was the drive back to the house! By the time we returned, we'd gone through two red lights, terrorized a farmer on his tractor, and missed a parked car by an inch!

Great-Aunt Abigail didn't seem to notice that anything was wrong.

My heart still in my mouth, I leaped out of the car and staggered over to Muttster. He wagged his bushy brown tail and licked my face, as if I'd been gone for ten years!

But he stopped in mid-lick when Great-Aunt Abigail climbed out of the car. "GRRRRRRRR," he growled ferociously, straining at his leash.

What is going *on* here? I asked myself.

Why does everything seem so different — so *wrong*?

I saw the eerie lights again that night. And the next night, too. Bigger and brighter than ever. Hovering in a circle over the woods.

As I pressed my face up against the window to watch them, I suddenly had a frightening thought. They looked just like the lights of the alien spaceship in my favorite movie, *Attack of the Pod People*.

49

I tried desperately to come up with another explanation for the lights. Streetlights? Not in Fairview. A plane? A plane couldn't hover like that. And I'd *never* seen a plane with lights that bright.

I felt a chill down my back as I realized there was no other explanation. Aliens had invaded Fairview. And they were landing in the woods near my great-aunt's house!

Wrapping my arms around myself to stop the chills, I found myself thinking about Great-Aunt Abigail. She seemed so different, so changed.

Had the aliens taken over Great-Aunt Abigail's mind? Just like in the *Pod People* movie?

I could hear Muttster start to bark down in the yard. Dogs have a sixth sense, I knew. Muttster sensed that Great-Aunt Abigail was possessed by an alien. That's why he had been barking and growling at her.

Suddenly gripped with fear, I turned away from the window.

Was I next? Would the aliens come after me next?

I had to get out of there. Run away. But where?

Mom and Dad were thousands of miles away. Should I call my best friend, Jessica, back home? She'd think I was joking. Besides, how could she help?

I needed someone closer. The police!

Trying not to make a sound, I crept down the

stairs to the phone in the kitchen. Great-Aunt Abigail — or *whoever* she was — had gotten there first.

She had her back to me. She couldn't see me. But I could hear her: "Don't worry, my niece doesn't know. Yes, yes, I told her to stay away from the woods. And she won't know anything until it's all over tomorrow night."

My palms started sweating, and I got that itchy feeling under my arms I always get when I'm really nervous.

"All over?"

Until *what* was all over? The alien invasion? Until Muttster and I had been taken off to some weird planet where they'd put us in cages?

I had to get back to my room — and fast. I turned back to the stairs. But the floorboards creaked loudly beneath me.

Great-Aunt Abigail whirled around to face me.

I gasped, and my mouth dropped open in horror.

My great-aunt's face was glowing green!

"Lucy — what are you doing up?" Great-Aunt Abigail demanded. She took a few steps toward me. I suddenly realized I was *terrified* of her.

"Uh . . . just going back to b-bed," I stammered, backing away.

I hurried up the stairs, my entire body trembling. I closed the bedroom door tightly and waited. Waited to hear Great-Aunt Abigail pad up the stairs and go into her room.

I knew I couldn't spend another minute in the house. I couldn't stay there with an alien from outer space.

Frantically, I pulled on jeans and a sweatshirt. I had to get to the police. I had to tell them about the aliens.

But would they believe me?

They will if I go to the woods and see the aliens first, I decided.

I know, I know. I wasn't thinking clearly. But I was having a major panic attack. And it seemed like the best idea at the time.

I sneaked silently down the stairs and out the back door. I should have woken up Muttster and brought him with me to the woods. But I was so out of my mind with fear, I didn't even think of him.

I ran across the backyard, heading to the woods. Nothing but darkness ahead. No lights hovering in the sky.

What was waiting for me in that darkness? Were there really aliens there? I needed to get a glimpse of them. Just a glimpse, so I could describe them to the town police.

The woods were dark, steamy, and wet. It was like plunging through a thick jungle. There was no path, so I had to push my way through, stumbling over fallen logs and marshy ground.

As I made my way, I kept hearing rustling noises on both sides of me.

Was I being followed? Was I being watched?

As I stopped to catch my breath, a light appeared up ahead. Swallowing hard, I moved toward it. The trees thinned out, and I found myself in a large clearing.

What were those sounds? Voices? Human voices?

Or alien voices?

I gasped as the bright lights washed over me. The white beam blinded me, captured me in a harsh spotlight.

I shielded my eyes as the light hovered over me, closing in, covering me, holding me helpless.

"Bring her here," I heard a deep voice order.

I felt hands tugging me.

I tried to pull away. But my captor was too strong.

"You can't take over my brain!" I shrieked. "I won't let you!"

"Cut the lights," another voice ordered.

The harsh lights dimmed to black. I could see smaller lights all around.

As my eyes adjusted to the darkness, I saw a man walk toward me. He wore a baseball cap and a long-sleeved Polo shirt over jeans.

"Young lady, I don't know what you're screaming about," he said. "But you can't just wander on to a film set. You just ruined a shot that took three hours to set up."

Film set? I opened my mouth to reply. But no sound came out.

"We asked the people in town to stay out of the woods," the man said sternly. "We're finishing our movie tomorrow. Then we'll be out of here."

"M-movie?" I took a deep breath, trying to get myself together. Suddenly, I heard dogs barking.

"The dogs are ready," a young woman carrying a clipboard announced. She raised a dog whistle to her lips. She blew into it. It made no sound that I could hear. But the dogs immediately barked louder.

That explains why Muttster has been barking all the time, I told myself. He keeps hearing the dog whistle from the woods.

Everything made sense now. Great-Aunt Abigail warning me to stay out of the woods. The bright lights. My great-aunt saying on the phone that it would all be over tomorrow night.

"I-I'm sorry," I told the man. "Really. I'm so sorry."

I felt like a total jerk.

I ran all the way home. Great-Aunt Abigail was waiting for me at the back door, her face tight with worry. "Lucy, where did you go? Where have you been? I was about to call the police."

I told her how sorry I was. And then the words just burst out of me. "I saw the lights. And Muttster was acting so strange. And your skin was green. And you drove so wildly. And the cookies were wrong. And — and — "

Great-Aunt Abigail wrapped me in a hug and held me till I stopped trembling. When I finally backed away, she was chuckling. "I guess my green mint julep facial mask would give *anyone* the creeps!" she declared.

I laughed, too.

"I should have told you about the movie folks," Great-Aunt Abigail said, shaking her head. "But I figured they'd be gone by tomorrow."

I started to say something. But she raised a hand to stop me. "I have more to explain," she said, frowning. "I have a confession to make, Lucy. I lost my glasses just before you arrived. And I've been trying to get along without them."

"That's why your driving was so wild?" I cried.

She nodded. "And that's why my cooking may have been a little off. It's so hard to see the ingredients."

We hugged each other again and shared a good laugh. "I can't believe you thought I was an alien from outer space!" Great-Aunt Abigail said. "You've seen too many movies!"

She was right. I felt like such a fool.

We had some hot chocolate. It didn't taste quite right, but I didn't complain. Then I made my way upstairs to go to sleep.

The night had grown cool, and I love sleeping

with the windows open. So I went to the linen closet to get an extra blanket.

As I pulled open the door, Great-Aunt Abigail's glasses tumbled out.

Terrific! I thought. Now she won't have to buy new ones.

I picked them up and carried them down the hall to her room. "Aunt Abigail?" I called.

The door was open a crack. I pushed it open and stepped inside. She stood with her back to me. "Aunt Abigail — look. I found your — "

My words choked in my throat as she turned to face me.

And I saw the four slimy tentacles waving at her sides. Her skin glowed bright green in the light from the dresser top. And her three fat, black lips made sucking sounds as she unrolled a long blue tongue.

"You found my glasses!" she croaked, reaching out all four tentacles toward me. "Thanks, Lucy."

GOOD FRIENDS

Jordan and his best friend, Dylan, hopped off the school bus and walked up Oak Street. "Want to ride bikes?" Jordan suggested.

"Yeah, okay," Dylan replied. "But I have to do my homework first."

Jordan rolled his eyes. Dylan was the only sixth-grader he knew who always did his homework the second he got home from school.

Jordan dropped his backpack on the front lawn and crossed the street. "Can't you do it later?" he asked.

Dylan kicked a pebble across the sidewalk. "No way. My mom will have a cow," he muttered.

Jordan sighed and pushed his bangs out of his eyes. "Then just tell her you did your homework in school, Dylan. She won't be home for hours. She won't know if you did it or not."

Dylan bit his bottom lip. "I don't know, Jordan," he said, lowering his voice. "What about — ?" He pointed toward his house.

"Who? Richard?" Jordan asked, making a face. "Will you forget about him already? Your older brother is a total jerk!"

Dylan shot a nervous glance toward the house. "Sshh! He'll hear you!"

Jordan folded his arms across his chest. "So what?" he demanded loudly. "Everyone knows Richard is a total jerk!"

Dylan gasped. "Come on, Jordan," he pleaded. "Be quiet! He'll *pound* me!"

Jordan shook his head. He couldn't believe Dylan was so scared of his brother. Richard was fourteen, and big and strong. But so what?

"Just forget about him, will you?" Jordan said. "Come on. Let's ride."

They rode their bikes around the neighborhood for a while. Then they stopped in Dylan's driveway to shoot some hoops. Dylan kept staring up nervously at his brother's bedroom window.

"I hope he leaves us alone today," he said to Jordan. "Ever since my mom put him in charge after school, Richard has been worse than ever. He acts like he's the king of the house."

"Oh, he's King all right," Jordan snickered. "King of the Jerks!"

Dylan laughed nervously and glanced back up to the window.

"Would you forget about him already?" Jordan said. "Come on, let's play. Show me your best slam dunk!"

Dylan dribbled the ball on the driveway. He was just about to shoot — when The Pest came skipping across the street.

The Pest was Ashley, Jordan's seven-year-old sister. Ashley plopped down on the sidewalk in front of Dylan's house and began playing with her Barbie dolls and talking to herself.

"Jaclyn, your hair is long and pretty like Barbie's!" Ashley said.

Jordan and Dylan exchanged glances, then cracked up. "Your sister is talking to her imaginary friend again," Dylan said, rolling his eyes.

"You're *sad!*" Jordan called out to his sister. "You're really *sad!*"

Ashley shot Jordan an angry look. "Shut up, dummy!" she screamed at him. "Jaclyn and I think that *you're* sad!"

"Where *is* Jaclyn?" Jordan demanded. "How come Dylan and I can't *see* Jaclyn? How come it looks like you're talking to yourself again?"

Ashley ignored her brother. "Don't pay any attention to them, Jaclyn," she said. "They're just acting dumb."

Dylan shook his head. "Come on, Jordo," he said softly. "Let's just play."

Jordan made a face at his sister, then grabbed the ball and took a jump shot. The ball hit the rim and bounced off.

"Hahaha!" Ashley burst out laughing. "Did you

see that, Jaclyn?" she cried. "Jordan missed an easy one."

"Ashley — get lost!" Jordan cried angrily. "And take your imaginary friend with you!"

Ashley dropped her dolls and ran up to him. "I told you, Jaclyn isn't imaginary!" she screamed. "She's real!"

"Oh, yeah?" Jordan shot back. "Then if Jaclyn is real, where is she standing?"

"Right here," Ashley replied, pointing to her left.

Jordan lobbed the ball at high speed in that direction. "Think fast, Jaclyn!" he shouted.

Ashley gasped. "No! Stop it! You'll hurt her!"

Jordan laughed and moved closer to his sister. "How come Jaclyn didn't catch the ball?" he teased.

"Because . . . because . . . you threw it too fast!" Ashley stammered.

"Where is she now?" Jordan demanded. "Let me try it again. This time, I'll aim for her head!" He and Dylan both laughed.

"You leave us alone! I'm telling!" Ashley whined. "Come on, Jaclyn. Let's go." She turned to leave.

"Come on, Jaclyn!" Jordan mocked in a whiny voice, trying to imitate his sister.

"Shut up, Jordan!" Ashley cried.

"Shut up, Jordan!" Jordan repeated.

"Cut it out!"

"Cut it out!" Jordan grabbed the air and pretended to hold somebody. "Hey, look, Ashley — I've got Jaclyn! She's my prisoner!"

Ashley balled her hands into fists. "Let her go! Let her go!"

"Hey, Dylan, bring me that rope from the garage. Let's tie Jaclyn to that tree!" Jordan cried, grinning.

Ashley screamed. "No! Stop! Jordan, let her go!"

Jordan kept laughing. "Wait! Maybe Jaclyn would like to help us practice our jump shots! We can hang a net on her head and use her face as a backboard!"

"I'm telling! I really am!" Ashley declared. She picked up her dolls and angrily ran down the driveway and across the street.

"Do you see what I have to put up with?" Jordan said, shaking his head.

Dylan started to answer. But an angry voice interrupted, shouting from the window above them. "Hey — loser!"

Jordan and Dylan raised their eyes to the upstairs window.

Dylan's brother, Richard, stuck his head out. "Dylan, did you do your homework yet?" he called down. "You'd better have it finished — or I'm telling Mom!"

Dylan nervously rolled the ball between his hands. "Just ignore him," Jordan whispered.

Dylan lifted the ball and tossed it up to the net. The ball missed the backboard completely.

Richard burst out laughing. "You really *are* a loser, Dylan! I could make that shot blindfolded. Who taught you how to play? Did your best friend, Jordan, teach you how to shoot like that?"

Jordan's face grew red. He opened his mouth to say something nasty. But Dylan's eyes pleaded with him not to.

"Please, Jordan," Dylan begged in a whisper. "Just ignore him! Please!"

"What did you say?" Richard shouted down from the window. "Are you talking to me, loser?"

Dylan cleared his throat. "No. Just leave me alone. I did my homework already. So just leave me alone."

Richard shook his head. "Try shooting with *both* hands!" he called down. Then he slammed the window shut with a loud thud.

Dylan hugged the ball tightly to his chest. His face was white. "He thinks he's so great," he muttered, his voice trembling.

"What a jerk!" Jordan exclaimed. "Why do you let him boss you around like that?"

Dylan shrugged. "Because he can beat me up," he admitted.

"Well, if he were my brother, I'd tie him to his

bed at night and tape his mouth shut!" Jordan said seriously.

Dylan laughed. "You always have the *best* ideas, Jordan!"

"What are good friends for?" Jordan replied.

Later, Dylan sat at his desk, slumped over his math book.

"I've got it!" Jordan cried suddenly, startling him.

"You've got what?" Dylan asked.

"The perfect trick to play on Ashley!" Jordan announced with a mischievous grin.

Dylan smiled and lowered his pencil. "What is it?" he asked eagerly. "Your tricks are always the coolest!"

"Thanks!" Jordan replied proudly. "Okay, here it is. You know how scared Ashley is of Axel and Foley, right?"

Dylan nodded. "Yeah, I don't like Richard's pet tarantulas much, either."

"Well," Jordan continued, grinning, "what if Axel and Foley somehow got loose?"

Dylan's eyes widened. "I don't know — "

"Oh, come on!" Jordan insisted. "Ashley would freak! I'll run up to her and scream, 'The spiders are loose! The spiders are loose! Run for your life!' Then, when Ashley runs out screaming, I'll tell her that I saw Axel swallow Jaclyn up whole!"

"Well . . ." Dylan hesitated. His friend's plans always scared him a little.

"Dylan, come on! It's perfect! Look at her!" Jordan pointed out the bedroom window. "My dopey sister is playing catch with her invisible friend right there in the front yard for everyone to see!"

Dylan peered out the window. "She does look pretty stupid," he admitted.

"Okay, so let's sneak into Richard's room, and — "

"Jordan, I don't know if this is such a good idea," Dylan said. "Richard will pound me for sure if we touch his spiders."

"Oh, stop worrying so much!" Jordan replied impatiently. "He'll never know! He's down in the den right now watching television. We'll be real quiet. No problem!"

Dylan peered out the window again and watched Ashley playing catch with her imaginary friend. "Okay. Let's do it," he agreed.

Jordan led the way to Richard's room. They crept inside and made their way to the tarantula tank.

"Go ahead," Jordan urged, whispering. "Pick them up. Hurry."

Dylan picked up the two tarantulas, one in each hand. They felt warm and hairy. They kind of tickled.

Tiptoeing silently, they made their way downstairs, sneaking past Richard in the den. Jordan pushed open the front door. They crept down the front steps and onto the driveway.

"This is going to be awesome!" Jordan whispered as they crept up behind Ashley.

Dylan held the tarantulas high above his head.

Ashley didn't hear them coming. She was laughing, calling out to her invisible friend, "Nice throw, Jaclyn!"

They tiptoed closer, until they were right behind her. One more step, and . . .

"DYLAN!" a voice roared from the porch.

Jordan and Dylan whirled around.

"It's Richard!" Dylan gasped in horror. Jordan saw his friend's face go white.

Richard moved toward them quickly, glaring furiously at Dylan.

"What are you doing out here with my tarantulas?" Richard demanded.

"I . . . uh . . . well . . ." Dylan stammered.

"I *know* what you're doing!" Richard accused angrily. "You're playing with Jordan and Ashley again, aren't you?"

Dylan stumbled backward as Richard moved closer. "Well . . ."

"Do you know what an *embarrassment* you are?" Richard cried. "You're just such a weird kid! Always playing by yourself and talking to yourself!"

"But — but . . . " Dylan sputtered.

Richard took the tarantulas from Dylan's hands. "Dylan, you're too old for imaginary friends," Richard said. "Forget about Jordan and Ashley. Okay? They don't exist. They're just in your mind. Imaginary friends are for babies!"

HOW I WON MY BAT

I guess you're admiring my swing, right? And you're admiring the baseball bat I'm holding.

Maybe you're wondering how I got this bat. There's a story behind it. That's for sure.

I was the power hitter on my junior high's baseball team. Our team went to the state finals every year, and I was the star.

You could read about me in the local paper all the time: "Michael Burns: He's Got the Power." "Michael Burns Wins It for Lynnfield . . . Again!"

That's me, Michael Burns. But now I wish I'd never even touched a baseball bat. Things are diferent now. I'm different.

How much time has gone by since the afternoon that changed my life? I'm not sure. But I can remember everything that happened as if it were yesterday. . . .

Baseball practice. We had just finished doing our warm-up exercises on the field. Coach Manning called out, "Hey, Mike! You're up at bat."

At the games, I always batted cleanup. Fourth in the lineup. That made sense. I was the best.

But this was only practice. And the coach liked to shuffle us around, to keep us on our toes.

I felt all my muscles go tight as I stepped up to the plate. You see, I had a problem. A big problem. I was in a real batting slump.

The last game we played, I struck out four times!

And the past few batting practices? Jimmy, the pitcher, would lob me the ball and I'd choke — swinging with everything I had as if they were fastballs.

Some power hitter, huh? I couldn't even connect. And everyone knew it. I was afraid my new nickname was going to be "Swing-and-Miss Mike!"

"Come on, Mike," Coach Manning called as I took a few practice swings. "Concentrate now. You know tomorrow's game with Lakeland is for first place."

"Yeah, Mike, don't mess up," Jimmy muttered from the pitcher's mound.

I hunched over the plate. The bat just didn't feel right. It felt heavy. Too heavy. "Relax," I told myself. "Just relax, and everything will be fine."

The pitch came. High. I let it go. "Strike!" Ron called from behind me.

I turned to him. "Since when does the catcher make calls?"

"Since when does the power hitter strike out every time?" he shot back.

Well, that did it. No way could I relax after that crack.

I tried to get my old swing back. But the bat felt even heavier. And I could see my teammates shaking their heads.

After about ten minutes of batting practice — where the best I could do was a little dribble right to the pitcher — the coach called in somebody else.

"Listen, Mike," he said, putting his heavy arm around my shoulder. "Why don't you go home and get some rest for tomorrow's game."

I thought he was being nice. But then he added in a sharp voice, "You'd better shape up, kid. This game is for all the marbles."

I trudged off the field feeling lower than a grounder to third.

"Hey, Mike. Hold up a second." I recognized the guy jogging toward me. It was Tom Scott, a local TV reporter.

School sports are a big deal in Lynnfield. But a TV reporter covering a practice? Wow!

"You feeling okay, Mike?" he asked me. "Are you doing anything to shake this slump?"

"I'm trying," I mumbled, feeling my face turn

red. "Really." I hurried into the locker room, feeling really embarrassed.

I showered and dressed in a hurry. I wanted to get out of there before the team finished practice. I knew I couldn't stand all the teasing I'd get.

A few minutes later, I stepped back outside and started toward the bike rack. I had my eyes on the ground, and I was deep in my unhappy thoughts. "I'd give *anything* to get out of this slump," I muttered to myself.

I didn't even see the strange-looking little man until I nearly tripped over him. "Oops. Sorry," I muttered.

He smiled at me. "I heard what you said. You just need a lighter bat," he said.

"Huh?" I squinted at him, startled.

The man wore a heavy, black wool suit. He had a tiny, round head, completely bald. His skin was so pale, he looked like a lightbulb!

Had this guy ever been outdoors?

"What did you say?" I asked him.

"You need a lighter bat," he repeated. His eyes were silvery. They crinkled as his grin grew wider.

I saw for the first time that he held a baseball bat in one hand. He raised it so that I could see it better.

It was shiny black wood. It had tape wrapped around the end. It looked as if it had been used before.

"It's very light — and very powerful," the man said. He let out a strange cackle, as if he had just told a joke.

"Wh-who are you?" I stammered, staring at the bat.

"I'm a sports fan," he said. With his free hand, he reached into his suit jacket pocket. He pulled out a business card and handed it to me.

It read: MR. SMITH, DIRECTOR. LYNNFIELD SPORTS MUSEUM.

I handed the card back to him. I stared at the bat. "You want to sell me this bat?"

He let out another cackle. He shook his shiny bald head. "I'll give it to you, Mike." His strange, silver eyes glowed excitedly.

Had I told him my name?

"It's a very good bat. You'll like it," he said. "Very powerful."

The bat didn't look very special to me. "You want to *give* it to me?"

He nodded. "Take it. Now. You just have to make one promise."

I knew there had to be a catch! "What promise?" I asked. Clouds rolled over the sun. The air turned cold. I felt a chill at the back of my neck.

"You have to promise you will return the bat to the museum — right after the game. You will not change clothes. You will not go home first. You will return it to me at the museum. Understood?"

71

He pushed the bat into my hands.

He's crazy! I thought. Why am I taking this bat? Am I *that* desperate to get over my batting slump?

Yes!

My hands wrapped around the bat. It didn't feel any different from the bat I had used that afternoon.

Then a chill passed through my body. Mr. Smith's ice-cold hand gripped my shoulder. "Remember," he said, "return the bat right after the game."

I nodded and slung the bat over my shoulder. Then I made my way to my bike and pedaled away as quickly as I could.

The next day was sunny and cool. A perfect day for baseball.

The locker room was noisy before the game. All the guys were talking and laughing. But I was sitting quietly, trying to psych myself up.

"Hey, Mike," Jimmy called, tossing me a water bottle. "We're behind you all the way. We're counting on you, man."

"Yeah." Ron gave me the thumbs-up. "We know you won't let us down."

I felt so nervous, the water bottle nearly slipped out of my hand. I took a long swig of water. "I can't strike out," I told myself. "I won't strike out."

And then it was time. We were up at bat.

In the dugout, Coach Manning called everyone to gather around for the new batting order. "I've made some changes," he began, staring right at me.

I knew what the coach meant, and so did everyone else. He was moving me from the cleanup spot. "Ron will bat fourth," he said, "and Mike will bat second."

Second? I could deal with that. I'd be able to show everybody that much sooner that I was still a winner.

Rick, the first guy at bat, hit a single.

My turn at the plate.

"I can't watch this," I heard Jimmy groan to Ron.

I picked up my new bat. All of a sudden it felt really light, just as the strange little man had said.

I carried it to home plate and took my stance.

This is weird! I thought. The bat started to tingle. Suddenly, I felt tiny vibrations all the way to my toes.

The pitch came — low and outside. "Strike!" called the umpire.

I let the second pitch go, too. Strike again.

I had to swing at the next one, no matter what. The bat tingled and vibrated in my hands.

The pitch was a fastball. I sucked in my breath and swung, trying to stay in control.

Crack!

The ball sailed high into the air. I shaded my eyes as I ran to first. But the ball flew so high, I couldn't see it. Was it going over the fence for a home run?

It was!

"It worked!" I shouted gleefully. "The bat worked!"

I jogged to second, my arms held high above my head in a victory sign. The third-base coach was grinning, waving me along.

My teammates charged over as I rounded third, cheering and thumping me on the back. Then I came home.

Lynnfield: 2. Two runs batted in for me.

The next inning, I hit an even higher home run.

Two innings later, I came to bat twice — and hit *two more* home runs!

That's the way it went every time I went to bat. I pounded out homer after homer. By the time I hit my seventh, the crowd was going *ballistic!*

Seven home runs broke the school record. And when I hit my ninth? That broke the state record!

The final score: Lynnfield: 19, Lakeland: 3. Not shabby. Not shabby at all.

Afterward, a crowd of people swarmed around me. Jimmy and Ron hoisted me on their shoulders, and Tom Scott, the TV guy, asked me questions while camera crews and photographers took pictures.

"Hey, Mike!" Ron waved me over after everything settled down. "We're all going to Pat's Pizza Place. You know, to celebrate. So come on, man — you're the star!"

I hopped on my bike. "Lead the way!" I cried, so excited about the game, I thought I might burst.

We rode off, still in our uniforms. The whole team was chanting, "Mike! Mike! Mike!"

It was a great feeling. But, suddenly, my heart sank. The bat! I had promised to return it right after the game. I had promised to deliver it back to Mr. Smith at the sports museum.

I slowed down, letting the other guys pass me by. They were still chanting my name as they disappeared around the corner. "Catch up with you later!" I called. I don't know if they heard me or not.

But I knew one thing for sure. I couldn't return the bat.

No way.

I had to keep it.

It was the greatest bat in the world. The bat had hit nine home runs in one game. I couldn't part with it. Promise or no promise — I had to keep it.

Standing over my bike, I gripped the bat in my hands, trying to decide what to do. My first thought was to ride home and hide the bat in my room. Mr. Smith didn't know where I lived. Chances are, he would never find me.

No. I decided that wasn't right.

I decided to go to the museum. To tell Mr. Smith the truth. That I *had* to have that bat. I'll offer to pay him for it, I decided. Any amount he wants. It's worth it.

I remembered the address from the business card. It took a long time to ride my bike there. The museum was in a strange part of town. Nobody on the streets. No cars. Nothing.

The museum was a low, gray building. Not too inviting. I parked my bike beside the entrance. Carrying the bat, I stepped inside.

What a cool place! I couldn't believe I'd never been there before. The enormous, bright room was filled with life-size sports displays.

Two players elbowed each other fiercely in a hockey display. The figures were made of wax or something. I couldn't *believe* their scary expressions.

I walked past a tennis display. A young man in tennis whites had his racket up, about to serve to another player. They looked so real, I expected to see the ball fly over the net!

I passed two high school basketball players going up for a rebound. Their muscles were straining. I could actually see beads of sweat running down their faces.

Cool, I thought, leaning on the bat as I studied the display. So cool!

The baseball display was under construction. Part of a diamond had been built, but there were no wax figures playing ball.

As I stared at the real-looking scene, Mr. Smith appeared from behind it. "Hello, Mike," he said, smiling. His bald head shone under the bright display lights. "Thanks for returning the bat."

I hesitated. "I . . . uh . . . can't return it," I stammered.

His silver eyes narrowed in surprise. "What?"

"I have to keep it," I told him. "It's the greatest bat in the world. I'll do anything to keep it, Mr. Smith," I pleaded.

He rubbed his pale chin. "Well . . ."

"Really," I insisted. "I really need this bat. I want to keep it forever!"

"Okay," he agreed. "You can keep it forever."

My mouth fell open. I was stunned. "You mean it? I can keep it?"

He nodded, smiling. "If that's what you want," he murmured. "Let me see your swing, Mike. Take a good swing, okay?"

I was so happy and grateful. I lifted the bat, started to show off my swing — and froze in a blinding flash of silver light.

And I've been standing here ever since. Frozen in place. The bat gripped tightly in my hands. About to take my best swing.

A lot of time has passed. I don't really know how much. I stare out at the cardboard backdrop, and I prepare to take my swing.

People visit the sports museum. They come over to the baseball display. And they stare at me.

They talk about how real I look. And what a great swing I have.

It makes me happy that they like my swing.

And, I guess I have one other thing to be happy about.

I get to keep the bat. Forever.

MR. TEDDY

"Mom, can I *please* get this teddy bear! Please? I'll never ask for another thing."

Willa clasped her hands together and gazed longingly at the stuffed teddy bear staring at her from the department store shelf.

Willa was a collector. She collected stuffed animals, dolls, posters, porcelain eggs — you name it. Every inch of her room was crammed with her collections.

"Mom, look at him!" Willa gushed. "Have you ever seen such cute little brown paws? And look at his big, round eyes. They're practically glowing."

Leaning on the counter, Gina, Willa's eleven-year-old sister, started to whine. "Mom! No fair! Willa already has enough stuffed animals to fill this whole store."

"So?" Willa shot back. "I can't help it if *your* room is bare, Gina."

Gina made a face at her older sister. "That's

because every chance you get, you beg Mom to buy you something else. 'Mom, get me this. Mom, buy me that,' " Gina mimicked.

"Girls! That's enough!" Mrs. Stewart cut them off. Willa and Gina glared at each other. "Willa, you're twelve. Aren't you getting too old for teddy bears?" her mother asked.

"I can't help it, Mom," Willa replied. "I want him. He's . . . not like any other stuffed animal I've ever seen."

"His eyes are weird," Gina commented.

"They are not!" Willa protested. But she knew Gina was right. She could almost feel the bear studying her with those huge eyes of his.

"Willa," her mother said. "There isn't any space left in your room. Where will you put it?"

"I'll put Old Bear on the shelf and sleep with this one," Willa replied.

Gina folded her arms. "What's wrong with Old Bear?"

"Nothing," Willa told her. "I just love this one." She pressed him against her cheek. "See how cuddly he is? Please, Mom?"

Mrs. Stewart hesitated. "Well . . ."

"Mom, that's not fair!" Gina wailed. "Willa's always getting stuff. What about my CD player?"

"Gina, a CD player costs a lot more than a teddy bear," her mother answered sharply. "That's something you can ask for on your birthday."

"Mom, please?" Willa said, still clutching the bear.

"Oh, all right," her mother said, sighing. "But this is *it*, understand, Willa?"

Willa threw her arms around her mother. "Oh, thank you, thank you, thank you, Mom."

On the other side of the counter, Willa could see Gina scowling at her.

"Sometimes I really hate you, Willa," Gina muttered.

Willa waved the teddy in Gina's face. "His name is Mr. Teddy, Gina," she announced. "And you'd better be nice to him."

As soon as Willa got home, she took Mr. Teddy up to her room to show him around. "Here we are," she announced, opening the door. Her room was done all in peach, her favorite color.

To the right of the door stood her dresser. On top of the dresser was her porcelain egg collection. Willa gently picked up each egg and told Mr. Teddy where it had come from. Next, she showed him all the rock star posters that covered her walls. Then she went through the two long shelves above the dresser crammed with stuffed animals.

When she finished with the animals, Willa took Mr. Teddy over to the doll collection in the other corner. Willa had been collecting dolls the longest, and had the biggest collection of anyone she knew.

Still clutching Mr. Teddy, Willa crossed the room to her bed. "Hello, Old Bear," she said. She reached onto the pillow and picked up her ragged old teddy bear — the one she'd slept with since she was a baby — and kissed him on top of his head. "You're going to sleep over here now," she said, crossing back over to the shelves. She pushed aside a stuffed unicorn to make room for Old Bear. "Sleep tight," she told him.

Gina poked her head into the room. "Who's in here?" she asked.

"No one," Willa replied.

"Then who were you talking to?"

"Nobody."

Gina's eyes lit up. "You were talking to your stuffed animals again, weren't you?" She started laughing at Willa.

"Shut up, Gina!" Willa snapped. "You're mad because you didn't get a CD player."

"I am not," Gina answered. "I'm mad because you have Mom wrapped around your little finger. Every time you ask for something, she buys it." She stormed out, slamming the door behind her.

Willa glanced down at Mr. Teddy. "Don't worry about Gina," she whispered, carefully placing him on her pillow. "I bet she wishes she had a special bear, too. But she doesn't. You're all mine, Mr. Teddy. All mine."

That night, Willa slept with Mr. Teddy hooked in her arm. At first it felt funny to sleep with something so soft and fluffy. All the fur on Old Bear had worn off a long time ago.

But Mr. Teddy seemed to be staring at her. Every time she turned or moved, she felt his big eyes watching her.

Willa woke up early the next morning. The sun had barely begun to rise. Outside, she could hear birds chirping.

Something didn't feel right. She lifted her head and stared down at her bed.

Where was Mr. Teddy?

She groped around her covers, but couldn't feel him anywhere. Where was he?

Willa pulled herself up, squinting in the dim light. Had Mr. Teddy fallen out of bed?

She peered down at the floor. Not there.

She shook her covers again, then leaned over to check underneath the bed. "Are you there, Mr. Teddy?" she called softly.

A sock and some dust balls stared back at her. Where could Mr. Teddy be?

Willa's eyes moved up her dresser, then over to the windowsill above the doll corner.

She caught her breath. Mr. Teddy sat propped up on the windowsill, staring back at her. His eyes seemed to be shining.

"Huh?" Willa murmured. "How did you get over there?"

She climbed out of bed and lifted him off the windowsill. "Mr. Teddy," she scolded. "What are you doing? Did you get up and move during the night?"

The bear's dark eyes glowed back at her.

"Stop staring at me like that!" Willa laughed. "You're giving me the creeps." She kissed the top of his head, then popped him back on her pillow.

"Maybe I woke up and put him there myself and don't remember," Willa said to herself.

At breakfast, she caught Gina staring at her. "What are *you* looking at?" she asked sharply.

"Nothing," Gina smirked.

"Did you come into my room last night?" Willa demanded.

"No," Gina replied, still smiling. "Why would I?"

The next night, before she fell asleep, Willa made sure Mr. Teddy was hooked firmly in the crook of her arm. It took her a long time to fall into a restless sleep.

She kept waking up and checking on Mr. Teddy. But he was always right where she left him, in the bend of her arm, watching everything with those big, dark eyes of his. In a funny way, Willa felt as if he were guarding her.

She woke up the next morning with a start. Immediately, she felt around for Mr. Teddy.

Gone again!

Willa glanced suspiciously at the windowsill. Not there, either.

She sat up in bed and began to search the room. Her eyes swept over the doll corner, the floor, then moved up the dresser.

"Hey, you!" Willa cried out when she spotted Mr. Teddy on top of the dresser.

"What's going on, bear? What are you doing over there?" She jumped out of bed and hurried over.

She gasped when she saw the two porcelain eggs. They lay smashed under the big teddy bear.

Mr. Teddy's eyes had an evil glow.

"Who did this?" Willa demanded. "Who broke these eggs?"

Willa tried to think. It couldn't be Mr. Teddy. He didn't climb the dresser and plop down on the eggs. No way.

So who *could* it be? The one person who was jealous of all her stuff.

"Gina!" Willa shouted furiously. "How could you *do* this?"

Willa stormed into Gina's room. Empty. Where was she?

Willa stomped back into the hall and stood at

the top of the stairs. "Gina! I'm going to get you for this!"

Her mother appeared at the bottom of the stairs. "Why are you shouting, Willa?"

"Where's Gina?"

"She left early for school," her mother said. "Remember? She has chorus practice."

Willa clenched her fists. "Wait till she gets home tonight," she growled. "She'll be singing a sad song when I get through with her!"

That afternoon Willa paced the front hall, waiting for Gina to return home. She paced back and forth, back and forth, checking out the window every time she passed it.

Finally she saw Gina coming up the front walk. She angrily pulled open the front door to greet her.

"I know it was you who smashed my porcelain eggs last night!" Willa uttered in a shaky voice. She blocked Gina's path.

Gina pushed her aside. "What are you talking about, Willa? Are you totally losing it?"

"You know what I mean," Willa insisted. She followed her sister to the stairs. "You broke my best eggs for no reason. Then you moved Mr. Teddy onto the dresser to make it look like *he* did it. What a sick, stupid joke."

Gina stopped. "I really don't know what you're talking about."

"Do too," Willa snapped.

It *had* to be Gina. Who else could it be?

"You're just trying to get me in trouble with Mom," said Gina. "Leave me alone, Willa. I'm warning you."

Later, when Willa went to bed, she shoved Mr. Teddy all the way under the covers. "I want you to stay down there tonight, okay?" she told him. She curled her body around his, then pulled her covers up to her neck.

Nobody could get Mr. Teddy out now, Willa thought. At least not without waking her up.

But Willa was wrong.

The moment she woke up the next morning, Willa reached under the covers for Mr. Teddy.

Gone again.

"Huh?" Willa sat up, wide awake. "What's going on?"

She let out a shriek when she saw her dresser. The drawers had all been pulled out and turned upside down. Her clothing had all been strewn in clumps and piles over the floor.

Angrily hurling herself out of bed, Willa kicked aside a pile of T-shirts. "Gina!" she shrieked. "I'm going to *murder* you for this!"

Glancing up, she saw Mr. Teddy. He grinned at her from the dresser top.

Willa grabbed him. "Why is this happening to me?" she screamed. "Tell me this is a dream!"

Mr. Teddy's eyes glowed brighter. Willa heaved him onto the bed.

She flew down the stairs and burst into the kitchen. Gina was eating a bowl of cereal. "Why did you do it, Gina?" Willa demanded, clenching her hands into tight fists. "Why? Why? Why did you sneak into my room, and mess it all up, and — "

Gina gazed up from her breakfast. "I haven't been near your room. Honest." A grin broke out on her face.

Willa let out a furious cry. "See, Mom? See? She's smiling."

Mrs. Stewart narrowed her eyes at Gina. "Have you been playing mean jokes on your sister?" she demanded.

"No! No way!" Gina screamed. "Why are you blaming me for something I didn't do? I just smiled because it's funny. But I didn't do anything! Really!"

Willa stared hard at Gina. "I know you're lying," she said softly. "You're a liar, Gina. A total liar."

"I am not!" Gina shouted. She scraped her chair back from the table and jumped up. "You're the liar!" she told Willa. "You're just trying to get me in trouble for no reason!" She turned and stormed out of the kitchen.

"Stay out of my room, Gina!" Willa called after her. "You'll be sorry! I mean it! I really do!"

* * *

That night before climbing into bed, Willa
shoved her dresser up against her door. "There,"
she said, pressing Mr. Teddy's soft body against
her arm. "That should keep Gina out of here. What
do you think, Mr. Teddy?"

Mr. Teddy's round, black eyes glowed back at
her.

She slept restlessly again that night. Feeling
hot, she kicked off her covers. She turned onto
one side, then the other. She had strange night-
mares.

When she woke up the next morning, before
she opened her eyes, she reached out for Mr.
Teddy.

Gone.

Willa's eyes shot open.

She screamed.

The dresser had been pushed to the middle of
the room.

She sat up, her heart pounding. "My — my
room!" she murmured.

Swallowing hard, she stood up. And gazed
around her room.

Her posters — they had all been ripped from
the walls and crumpled onto the floor.

Willa's eyes moved to the shelves. To her
stuffed animals. A cold, sick feeling spread
through her stomach.

Nearly all of the animals had been pulled apart.

Shredded. Bits of them lay strewn across the room. A tail here. A piece of stuffing there.

Their eyes had been torn out of their heads. Their arms and legs ripped from their bodies.

Willa staggered to her doll corner. Every doll had been broken and torn apart. They lay in a heap of arms, scraps of clothing, broken heads, patches of hair.

"Hey!" Willa raised her eyes to the top of the shelf. Mr. Teddy stood there triumphantly, his eyes glowing happily. In one raised paw, he held an arm from one of her dolls.

"No!" Willa murmured. "No. Please — no!"

Mr. Teddy suddenly toppled forward. His outstretched arms reached for Willa's throat.

Willa let out a shriek and dived out of his way.

The bear landed on the floor with a soft thud.

Willa spun around. Tripping over parts of dolls and stuffed animals, she plunged out of her room. Down the stairs. Into the kitchen.

"Willa! What is it? What's wrong?" demanded her mother.

"Mom! Come up to my room!" she sobbed. "Everything I own! All my dolls, my animals. Gina wrecked it all!" she cried furiously.

"Huh?" Mrs. Stewart's face twisted in surprise. "Gina?"

"Yes! Gina!" Willa declared. "She broke into my room last night, Mom. She wrecked everything! Everything!"

90

"But that's impossible!" Willa's mother cried. "Gina wasn't home last night, Willa. Don't you remember? She had a sleep-over at Maggie's house."

Willa pressed her hands against her face. The room began to spin wildly.

That's right, she remembered. Gina wasn't home last night.

"Nooooo!" She backed out of the kitchen, hands against her cheeks, shaking her head.

She didn't want to believe it. It couldn't be. But there was no other explanation.

She ran blindly up the stairs. She grabbed Mr. Teddy off the floor. His eyes glowed up at her as Willa frantically ripped him to pieces.

"It *was* you, after all, wasn't it?" she cried, tearing off his arms, pulling out his white stuffing, letting it fly over the room. "It was you! You! You!"

With a cry of fury, Willa tore off Mr. Teddy's head. "I hate you!" she shrieked. She tossed the head out the open window. "Evil thing! Now you're gone! You can do no more evil!"

Gasping for breath, her heart thudding, Willa stumbled across the room and pulled raggedy Old Bear off the shelf. She hugged him tightly. "You're all I've got left, Old Bear. Everything else was destroyed by that evil thing."

She clutched Old Bear gratefully. "From now on, it's just you and me."

Willa didn't see the pleased smile form on Old Bear's mouth. She didn't see his eyes begin to twinkle merrily.

Next time, Old Bear thought to himself, *maybe you won't be so quick to get rid of me, Willa. Maybe you've learned your lesson. You can't put me away on a shelf. Not me. I'm your bear. And I'm going to be with you for the rest of your life.*

CLICK

My name is Seth Gold, and I'm twelve. My hobby is channel-surfing on the TV. At least, that *used* to be my hobby.

Why did I sit for hours, clicking from channel to channel with the remote control? I guess I loved the feeling of power it gave me.

A boring show? *Click* — on to the next. A loud commercial about sinus headaches? *Click* — on to something better.

Sometimes I tried to imagine what life was like when people had to get up and walk over to the TV every time they wanted to change the channel. But it was just too *awful* to think about.

One day, my dad came home from work carrying a package about the size of a shoebox. He plunked it down on the kitchen table. "Wait till you see this!" he exclaimed, removing the wrapping.

My four-year-old sister, Megan, shoved past

me. "What is it? What is it? Let me see!" she begged.

I read the big black letters on the box:

UNIVERSAL REMOTE

"I got a great deal on this," Dad explained. "I was on my way home from work, and I passed a little store I'd never seen before. It was going out of business. This thing was only six dollars. Great, huh?"

"What does it do?" I asked, pulling it carefully out of the box.

"It's just like our regular remote control, except it works everything," Dad explained. "It will work the TV, the VCR, the CD player. If we had a laser disc player, it would work that, too."

"Wow!" I exclaimed, excited. "Can I try it?"

"Sure, Seth," Dad replied. "Just put some batteries in it."

I took some AA batteries out of the kitchen junk drawer and loaded them into the chamber. Then I examined the remote. It was slender and black. It fit nicely into my hand. And it had a million buttons on it. This was going to be *awesome!*

I ran up the stairs to the den.

"Don't watch TV for too long!" my mother shouted after me. "You have homework — remember?" But I was already gone.

For the next hour, I fooled around with the new remote. It was really excellent. I could go back and forth between a videotape and the TV. I could play a CD while watching the Weather Channel with the sound turned off. It looked as if the weatherman were singing!

Megan wandered in. "I want to watch a cartoon tape," she said.

"Not now," I told her. "I'm busy."

"But I *want* to!" she insisted.

"Not now, Megan! Beat it!"

"I'm telling!" she whined.

"You are not!" I cried, reaching to stop her.

To my surprise, she grabbed the remote control out of my hand. Then she pulled back her arm and flung the new remote across the room. It crashed into the radiator and fell to the floor.

"Now look what you did!" I shrieked angrily.

I picked up the remote from the floor and shook it. It rattled. It hadn't rattled before. I clicked it at the TV.

Nothing happened.

"You jerk!" I cried. "Now we can't watch anything!"

"Sorry," Megan replied softly. She stuck her thumb into her mouth and backed slowly out of the room.

I sat down on the sofa and went to work on the remote. Using a quarter, I pried off the back and studied the insides. Not much in there except for a few chips and wires. I wiggled things as much as I dared, and then closed it up.

Holding it up to my ear, I shook it.

No rattle.

I pointed it at the TV. *Click*. It worked again!

Ten minutes later, I was busily channel-surfing when my mother stormed into the room. "Seth — I am very disappointed in you! I *told* you not to watch for long, and there are chores to be done in this house, and your sister tells me you won't let her have a turn, and — "

On and on she yelled, shaking her head. I tried to tune her out. But she was yelling louder and louder.

So I pointed the remote at her and pushed MUTE. It was a joke. Just a dumb joke.

But the most amazing thing happened. Mom was still yelling — but no sound came out. *I had really muted her!*

I pushed the button again. " — And your room is a mess, and your homework isn't getting done, and — "

Click. I muted her again. She continued yelling silently.

Awesome! This was really awesome! I could mute my own mother with the new remote control!

" — So you'd better start shaping up, mister," she finished. She turned and stormed out of the room.

"Wow!" I cried out loud. Sitting on the edge of the sofa, I stared at the buttons on the remote.

A few seconds later, our beagle, Sparky,

walked into the room. "Here, boy," I said. Sparky trotted over and started scratching himself behind the ear with his back leg.

I stared down at the remote again. I had to try it once more.

I saw a button labeled SLOW MOTION. I pointed the remote at Sparky, pressed the button, and held it.

Sparky started scratching himself very, very slowly. I could see his lips flapping as his head twisted slowly back and forth. His ears floated around in the air.

"Unbelievable!" I whooped. I let go of the button, and Sparky started scratching himself at normal speed again.

I can control the *world* with this remote! I told myself. I was so excited, I nearly dropped it again!

"Dinner!" Mom called from downstairs.

"Be right down," I shouted. I tucked the remote in my jeans pocket. I wasn't going to let it out of my sight. Then I charged down the stairs.

I was too excited to focus on eating my tuna casserole. I picked at my dinner, thinking about the remote, feeling it in my pocket.

My mother frowned as she cleared the plates. "Well, Seth," she said, "maybe you'll be more interested in dessert."

I glanced at the bowl. Chocolate pudding. My favorite.

Mom spooned it into plates, and I gobbled down my portion.

Then I had a *brilliant* idea. I quietly pulled out the remote and studied the buttons under the table. Ah — there it was: REWIND. I pushed the button and held it.

In rapid motion, Mom, Dad, and Megan *un*-ate their pudding!

I kept rewinding until Mom appeared with the bowl of pudding. Then I let the button go. "Well, Seth," she said again, "maybe you'll be more interested in dessert."

Then we all had pudding again!

"You bet," I said, gobbling down my second portion.

Ha! This was excellent! When I was done, I pushed REWIND again, and then one more time — until I'd had four dishes of chocolate pudding. I was stuffed!

The next morning, I carried the remote to school with me. I knew I shouldn't be messing around with it. But I couldn't help myself. It was too much fun.

After the first bell rang, it was time for the flag salute. I decided I had heard it enough times. So I muted it.

Everyone sat down. "And, now," said Ms. Gifford, "you're going to have a pop quiz in geography, you lucky people." She started passing out papers.

Oh, no! A pop quiz! I had been so busy with the new remote, I hadn't done the homework! I didn't know *anything* about South America!

I swallowed several times, thinking hard. Then I remembered the remote, and I relaxed. I had a plan.

Ms. Gifford finished passing out the papers. "Okay, everyone," she said. "You'll have twenty minutes. Good luck."

I took a quick glance at my test paper. It was full of questions I knew nothing about. The capital of Brazil? Not a clue.

But I wasn't worried. I doodled on my notebook while everyone else got busy answering the questions.

Nearly all the time had passed. "Thirty seconds left," announced Ms. Gifford.

I waited another fifteen seconds. Then I took the remote out of my pocket. I hit FREEZE-FRAME.

Everybody froze. Ms. Gifford stopped in the middle of a yawn, glancing out the window. Mickey Delaney froze in the middle of scratching his nose. Annie Schwartz, the best student in the class, froze in the middle of putting her pencil neatly down on the desk.

I stood up and strolled over to Annie's desk. I took my test paper with me. I peered over Annie's shoulder at her answers.

"San Salvador . . . okay. Andes Mountains . . .

okay . . ." I wrote all of Annie's answers onto my test sheet. Then I strolled back to my desk, sat down, and hit the FREEZE-FRAME button again.

Everybody snapped back into motion. "Okay, everyone," said Ms. Gifford. "Pencils down."

I set my pencil down, making a great show of looking exhausted. Then I passed my paper up to the front. This was really cool!

After the test, I looked for more ways to have fun. I fast-forwarded the teacher and the entire class for a while. I slow-motioned the principal when she came to talk to the teacher. Then I froze the whole class again.

When the teacher squeaked her chalk on the blackboard, I turned the volume way up. Finally, the bell rang for lunch. I couldn't wait to go down to the lunchroom — a whole new place to have fun.

The lunchroom was the usual zoo — everyone yelling and laughing, straw wrappers and juice boxes flying everywhere, kids falling off their chairs, dropping their lunch trays.

Mr. Pinkus, the lunchroom monitor, ran around yelling at everyone to sit down. I pointed the remote at him and froze him in his tracks.

Then I stepped into the food line. I took a cheeseburger, a salad, and two desserts.

"You can't have two desserts," said the lunchroom lady. "You know that."

I didn't even think twice. I pointed the remote

at her and punched the MUTE button. She continued to lecture me silently.

Quite pleased with myself, I continued down the line and picked up a carton of milk. Before I went to sit down, I pointed the remote at the lunchroom lady again and pressed MUTE to turn her voice back on.

Nothing happened.

I pressed the button again. She was still talking without making a sound. I banged the remote against my tray and tried again. But she still didn't get her voice back.

Well, it really isn't a tragedy if that lunchroom lady is muted for a while, I thought to myself. I never liked her anyway.

I figured the remote must need a little jiggling. I'd get it to work. I reached over to take another dessert.

But as I set the plate of pie down on my tray, my blood turned to ice. The remote wasn't there!

Breathing hard, I tried to think. Where was it? I had set it on the tray, hadn't I? I swallowed hard, feeling my panic rise.

"Freeze, Seth!"

I glanced up to see Danny Wexler, a big, freckle-faced, redheaded eighth-grader, standing a few feet away, pointing the remote at me!

"Danny — don't touch that!" I pleaded. "Don't press any buttons!"

Danny grinned at me. "Why not? Hey, why do

you have a remote control in school, anyway?" He moved his finger over the buttons, deciding which one to push.

"Don't touch it!" I begged. I dove for him and snatched it out of his hand.

"Hand it back, Seth," Danny growled. His eyes narrowed. His expression turned mean. He moved toward me with his hand outstretched.

In a panic, I hit the FREEZE-FRAME button. And froze him.

I started to back away. But a girl's startled cry made me stop. "Hey, what's going on? Why is Danny frozen like that?"

Melissa Fink stood staring at us. I realized in horror that she could see Danny, could see what was going on. Other kids were starting to crowd around.

"What is that?" Melissa demanded. She tried to pull the remote out of my hand.

"Don't touch it!" I warned. "Please!"

"What is going on here?" A woman's voice burst in. I glanced up to see the principal. "What's all this commotion?"

She saw the remote in my hand. "Seth, let me see that."

In a total panic, I pushed FREEZE-FRAME and froze her.

The lunchroom filled with frightened shouts. "Seth froze the principal! Somebody — help! Seth froze the principal!"

A big crowd moved around me. I started to back away.

I pressed the FREEZE-FRAME button again to unfreeze the principal.

But it didn't work. She stayed still as a statue.

My brain was whirling. The whole room started to spin. The shouts and cries of the other kids made it hard to think straight.

What had I done?

What if I can't unfreeze her? I thought, my entire body trembling. What if I can't unfreeze Danny or Mr. Pinkus?

Would they stay like that forever?

I knew I was in trouble now. *Major* trouble.

"Get Seth!" someone shouted. "Get that thing away from him!"

I turned and ran for the lunchroom door. Kids came running after me. "Stop him! Stop him!" they shouted.

I turned back and pointed the remote at them. I started pushing buttons frantically.

I didn't know what I was doing. I was so frightened. So totally panicked.

My heart pounded. My stomach was doing wild flip-flops.

I pushed button after button.

None of them worked. None of them did anything.

"Stop Seth! Stop him!" The crowd continued to chase me.

I pushed another button. Another button.

Not working. Nothing worked. And then I pushed the button marked OFF.

"Hey — !" I cried out as the world went black.

I blinked several times. But the darkness didn't lift.

It was silent now. Silent and black.

I'm all alone, I realized.

No shouting kids. No kids at all. No school. No light.

No picture. No sound.

A faint glow in my hand made me raise the remote control. I brought it close to my face. A small red light blinked steadily.

Squinting into the blinking light, I read the words beneath it: BATTERY DEAD.

BROKEN DOLLS

"You broke my doll!" Tamara Baker screamed.

"I did not!" Neal, her seven-year-old brother, protested. "The arm fell off. It wasn't my fault!"

Tamara grabbed the doll from his hand. The slender pink arm fell to the floor. "That's the third doll you broke, Neal!" she cried. "Why can't you keep your paws off my doll collection?"

"Aw, you've got plenty more," her brother muttered, pointing to Tamara's shelves and shelves of dolls.

"You could at least say you're sorry," Tamara scolded.

"Sorry," Neal said softly. And then a grin spread across his face as he added, "NOT!" He turned and ran out of Tamara's room.

She angrily slammed her door. She replaced the broken doll on its shelf, shaking her head. Then she walked to the mirror to brush her hair.

Tamara studied her reflection. She was twelve, and her face was longer and thinner than ever before. That was fine with Tamara, who wanted to look older.

She had large brown eyes. They were her best feature. Her skin was tanned, her nose was small and straight and, best of all this year — no braces! Tamara smiled. She was satisfied, except for her hair!

Tamara's hair was a long, dark, wavy mass that had always refused to be put in any normal style. Tamara frowned and tugged at it. I have a bad-hair day *every* day! she thought glumly. She brushed it back and jammed a couple of barrettes in it.

"Tamara, are you coming?"

She heard her dad calling impatiently from downstairs. He hated waiting. He was taking the family to the crafts fair at the fairgrounds. And he insisted on getting there when the fairgrounds opened at ten A.M.

Tamara opened her door and stepped on something squishy. It made a squeaking sound, and Tamara jumped a mile. Then she spotted Neal peeking out his door, laughing his head off.

"I scared you! I scared you!" he crowed.

Tamara picked up the object. It was a bath toy inside a sock, placed just where Tamara would have to step. She aimed and threw it at Neal's laughing face. He bolted for the stairs, and she chased after him.

"Children! Children!" Mrs. Baker cried as the two circled around her. "Stop this right now!"

"She started it!" Neal claimed in his whiniest voice.

"Mom — he broke another one of my dolls!" Tamara said.

"Stop it! Just stop it!" their mother ordered. "Get in the car, both of you."

The car ride seemed to take forever. Tamara sat in the backseat with Neal. Neal had never been able to sit still for more than ten seconds. He squirmed and bounced and stretched his neck to see out all the windows at once. It drove Tamara crazy.

Once they were at the fairgrounds, Neal went wild. He wanted to see everything and be everywhere at once.

"Tamara," Mrs. Baker said, "your dad and I want to see the ceramics. But I don't want Neal around things that can break."

"Good thinking, Mom," Tamara replied, rolling her eyes.

"So why don't you take him for a half hour, and then meet your father and me at the information booth after that?" Mrs. Baker suggested.

"ME take Neal?" Tamara howled in horror. "What do I look like? A wild-animal trainer?"

"No," Neal giggled. "You look like the wild animal! Hahahaha!"

Tamara could see that she was trapped. "Okay, I'll do it," she grumbled. "Come on, you little monster."

Tamara held Neal's hand in a "grip of death" so he couldn't get away. She wished she had a pair of handcuffs. She strolled around looking at exhibits, ignoring Neal's nonstop chatter.

Tamara wasn't much of a crafts person. Her mom was the "craftsy" one. Mrs. Baker couldn't look at a simple T-shirt without wanting to put rhinestone studs on it.

Still, Tamara enjoyed walking through the booths. There were quilts, clay pots, lots of handmade jewelry, and carved wooden toys that got even Neal's attention.

"Wow! How does this wooden popgun work?" Neal asked.

Tamara wasn't too interested in popguns. She turned to the booth across the aisle.

And saw the dolls.

There were at least fifteen or twenty of them. And they were strikingly human looking.

The dolls all had different faces, different expressions. One looked sweet, another pouting. The next was crying. Another was asleep. On and on, like a quiet nursery.

Tamara stared from doll to doll. They were so real looking. She thought if she touched one, the doll would feel warm, not cold like a regular doll. She reached out . . .

"Do you like them?" a raspy voice called from right behind her.

Tamara jumped. She turned and faced the oldest woman that she had ever seen. Her withered face was lined with deep crags. Her white hair hung down stiff as straw. Her eyes were narrowed slits.

"Did you make these dolls?" Tamara asked.

"Every one, dearie."

"I've never seen dolls like these before. They're so *real*!"

"No two are the same," the old woman replied. "and they're perfect in every detail. Go ahead, take a closer look."

Neal padded over to Tamara. "I'm hungry," he whined.

"I'll get you something in a minute," Tamara snapped.

"Aren't you *precious*!" the old lady crooned at Neal. "Quite the little man. I think there may be a cookie around here for such a nice boy."

Neal perked up at the mention of a cookie. Tamara turned back to the doll she'd been studying. It was wearing a dark purple dress with white trim.

She picked it up. "Wow. It weighs as much as a real baby, too," she said. "That's incredible."

Tamara set the doll down and turned around. As she did, she thought she saw the old lady put

109

her hand on Neal's head. The gesture was odd and formal, almost like a blessing.

Strangest of all was the look on Neal's face. He stood still. And quiet.

Tamara grabbed Neal's hand, harder than she intended, and pulled him away from the doll booth. "Come on. We've got to go," she said. "Thank the lady for the cookie."

"Thank you," Neal mumbled through a mouth full of crumbs.

Tamara and Neal met their parents, and the four of them walked around the exhibits together. They didn't go past the doll booth again.

When Mr. Baker had had enough, and Mrs. Baker had bought enough goodies to keep the entire family in puff-paint heaven through Christmas, they all piled into the family car and headed home.

Neal didn't squirm the way he had on the way to the crafts fair. In fact, he didn't do much of anything. He sat back in his seat, staring straight ahead.

Mrs. Baker noticed Neal's unusual quiet behavior as soon as they got home. She felt his forehead. "Ted, he's running a fever," she told her husband.

"Probably all the excitement today," Mr. Baker replied. "I'll get the baby aspirin. Neal, get into bed."

"I don't want to go to bed. It's daytime," Neal protested. But he went upstairs anyway.

Mrs. Baker got Neal into his pajamas and brushed her hand over his head lovingly. Tamara went upstairs just as Mrs. Baker pulled her hand away, chuckling.

"What have you gotten into, young man?" she asked, wiping something off her hand. "You've got some kind of goop in your hair."

"Dolly jelly," Tamara heard Neal mumble, before he drifted into a feverish sleep.

Later in the afternoon, Neal was covered in a light rash. His face was pale, washed out.

"Looks like an allergy, Marge," Mr. Baker decided. "What did he eat today?"

"Oh, Ted," Mrs. Baker replied, sighing. "What *didn't* he eat!"

Tamara felt bad that her brother was sick. She went to his room to sit with him for a while.

He looked so pale. As if his face were fading away.

She placed her hand on his forehead. It felt really hot. Neal was mumbling something in his sleep. She listened.

"No dollies. Don't want to be a dolly. No dolly jelly. No."

Dollies?

Tamara remembered the doll lady. The cookie.

Maybe the cookie had something in it that had made Neal sick.

She remembered watching the old woman place her hand on Neal's head. Dolly jelly . . .

"Mom, I'm going out for a little while, okay?" Tamara said, pulling on her jacket.

"Where are you going?"

"Just for a bike ride." Tamara hurried out the back door.

She jumped on to her bicycle and began pedaling furiously. The fairgrounds were a couple of miles away. And she didn't know how late the crafts fair stayed open.

She arrived at the fairgrounds just as the gates closed. "Well, I'm here," she told herself "*Now* what do I do?"

People were packing up their crafts. Closing their booths.

Tamara saw the doll lady step out from one of the crafts areas. She was carrying a box. Tamara watched carefully as the old woman took the box to a trailer marked EXHIBITORS ONLY.

Staying in the shadows, Tamara crept toward the trailer. She watched. The doll maker stepped out of the trailer. She kept walking back and forth, carrying one box at a time into the trailer.

Tamara waited until the old woman was out of view. Then she took a deep breath, and sneaked into the trailer.

Her heart fluttering in her chest, Tamara

searched the trailer. She kept remembering Neal mumbling about the dollies, and "dolly jelly."

Glancing at the trailer door, she opened several boxes marked "dolls" and peered inside. To her surprise, these were not the dolls she'd seen on display.

The faces on these dolls were completely blank.

Tamara shivered. There was something creepy about a doll without any face at all. The smooth white heads stared up at her like ghosts.

With a shudder, Tamara opened another box. This doll had a pale face, so pale she could barely make out its features. She touched the doll's smooth head and her hand came away smeared with the same goop that was in Neal's hair.

Dolly jelly.

"Ohh!" Tamara cried out as the doll's features darkened. Came clearer. And she recognized Neal's eyes. Neal's pointy nose. Neal's mouth.

"Wh what's happening?" Tamara stammered out loud. She gaped at the doll in horror.

The features darkened some more. Neal's face was growing clearer on the doll head.

Then she remembered how pale her brother had looked, lying in his bed asleep. How his face had appeared to be fading away.

"What is the old woman doing?" Tamara wondered aloud, frozen in sudden horror. "I've got to stop her!"

"Sssssstop her," a voice said.

Tamara gasped and spun around. Was it the old doll maker?

No. No one was at the trailer door. Where did the sound come from?

The closet.

"Sssstop her," a tiny voice repeated.

Swallowing hard, Tamara pulled open the closet door with a trembling hand.

Dolls. Crammed into the shelves.

The dolls from the crafts fair.

But they couldn't be dolls because they were moving! Reaching out their tiny, pink arms to Tamara!

"No!" Tamara shrieked. "You can't be alive. You *can't* be!"

She shrank back from their outstretched arms. "Don't touch me! Don't!" she pleaded.

Neal. She had to help Neal.

Tamara snapped back to her senses. She slammed the closet door shut. Then she grabbed the doll with Neal's features and darted out of the trailer.

"Going somewhere, dearie?" The old doll maker grinned at Tamara.

"Stay away from me!" Tamara cried breathlessly. "I've got the doll. My brother's doll! And I'm going to the police!"

The old woman's eyes sharpened. "Why don't you come inside, and we'll talk about it?" she said softly.

114

"No way!" Tamara exclaimed. "I saw your dolls. I know what you're doing!"

The old lady started toward Tamara, walking slowly but deliberately. Her face was hard and evil. "You don't know what I'm doing," she said through clenched teeth. "Your world has no idea of my ancient arts."

Tamara suddenly felt dizzy. What did she mean "your world"? Just how old *was* this woman?

The doll maker reached into her sweater and pulled out a container. Tamara recognized the goop that Neal had called "dolly jelly."

"I think it's time for you to go away, dearie," the old lady said quietly. "Young people disappear so often in this century. You'll just be one more. . . ."

The doll maker smeared a dab of the greasy goop on her fingers. Then she moved toward Tamara, mumbling some kind of chant.

Tamara struggled to move. But she couldn't.

She felt like a bird being hypnotized by a snake. The old woman looked like a cold, unblinking snake, slithering closer . . . closer . . .

"No!" Tamara shrieked — and dove forward. The sound of her own voice gave her strength.

She grabbed the jar of goop from the old woman's hand. Then she spun around and started to run.

"Give that back!" the doll maker called after her.

Tamara saw a small wading pool at the edge of the fairgrounds. She raised the jar of goop — and heaved it into the pool.

"You fool!" the old woman wailed. "You fool! What have you done?"

Tamara stared in disbelief as the pool water began to bubble and hiss. Choking clouds of black smoke rose up from the pool. The water turned green, then blue, then red. It swirled up in angry waves. Then splashed down hard under the billowing black smoke.

When Tamara turned back, the old woman had vanished.

She heard happy shrieks and cheers from the trailer. Were the dolls celebrating in there?

She didn't have time to find out. She ran to her bicycle and started to jam the Neal doll into her bike pack.

But to Tamara's surprise, the doll no longer looked like Neal. Its face was smooth and blank.

With a shiver that shook her whole body, Tamara tossed the doll as far as she could. Then she furiously pedaled home.

"Tamara, where on earth have you been?" Mrs. Baker scolded. "And just *look* at you! You're a mess!"

"Sorry, Mom," Tamara mumbled. "I'll clean up for supper."

Neal popped into the kitchen. He grinned at

Tamara. "You look like you've been playing in the mud!" he exclaimed. "Piggy! Piggy!"

"Neal! You're all right!" Tamara cried joyfully. She dropped to her knees and gave him an enthusiastic hug.

"Do you believe it?" Mrs. Baker said. "All of a sudden, his fever dropped, and he was his old self again."

"His old bratty self," Tamara laughed, ruffling Neal's hair. "Well, that's just fine with me!"

Everything was back to normal. Tamara decided to forget about the old doll maker. And the frightening, living dolls.

She forced the old woman out of her mind — until one night a few weeks later.

Her parents had gone out. Tamara was baby-sitting Neal.

Someone knocked on the front door.

"Who's there?" Tamara called out.

No reply.

"Who's there?" she repeated.

Still no reply.

Tamara peered out through the front window. A dark, moonless night. She didn't see anyone.

Curious, she pulled open the front door. And found a package on the front stoop. "Hey — !" She stared out at the dark street.

Who delivered this?

She carried the box inside and started to unwrap the brown paper.

"Is it for me?" Neal came hurrying into the living room. "Is it a present? For me?"

"I don't know," Tamara told him, struggling to tear off the wrapping.

A plain box was inside. She pulled open the lid.

And stared at a doll. An ugly doll. A doll with strawlike white hair. A craggy, wrinkled face. Narrow, squinting eyes.

"Ohh." Tamara recognized the doll instantly. It was the old woman. The doll maker.

She's followed me, Tamara realized.

She's found me.

She's here in my house with all of her evil.

Tamara felt cold all over. Her breath seemed to freeze as she stared in horror at the ugly, frightening doll.

She nearly dropped the box. What am I going to do? What can I do?

The idea popped into her mind.

She handed the doll to Neal. "Bet you can't break this one!" she told him.

"Huh?" He gaped at the doll, then back at Tamara.

"I dare you to break this one!" Tamara said.

"You dare me?"

Tamara nodded. "Bet you five dollars you can't."

"It's a bet!" Neal replied. He went to work on the doll.

A VAMPIRE IN
THE NEIGHBORHOOD

We knew there was something different about Helga the first time we saw her.

For one thing, she had that strange name. Helga. Such an old-fashioned name.

Helga looked old-fashioned, too. She wore the same black skirt to school every day. Old looking, and kind of worn, with no style at all.

My friend Carrie and I were sitting in the back of Miss Wheeling's sixth-grade class the first day Helga came to school. "Check her out, Maddy," Carrie whispered, motioning with her eyes.

I turned to the front of the room and stared at the timid-looking girl talking with Miss Wheeling. With her tight, black ringlets of hair and her pale gray blouse tucked into her black skirt, the girl looked as if she had stepped out of an old movie.

"This is Helga Nuegenstorm," Miss Wheeling announced. "She is new to our school, and I'm sure you will all make her feel at home."

Helga lowered her eyes to the floor. Her skin

was so pale, as if it had never seen the sunlight. And she was wearing lipstick. Black lipstick.

"She's weird," Carrie whispered.

"She's kind of pretty," I replied. "I've never seen anyone who looked like that."

Later, Carrie, Yvonne, Joey, and I took our usual table in the lunchroom. The four of us are really good friends. We have been friends for a long, long time. We sit together in the lunchroom every day.

"Did you see the new girl?" I asked. The four of us were tossing an apple back and forth across the table to each other.

"Isn't she weird?" Carrie asked.

Yvonne and Joey nodded. "She's so pale, but she wears that yucky black lipstick," Yvonne said.

"Maybe she isn't wearing lipstick," Joey joked. "Maybe those are her lips!"

"Do you know where she lives?" I asked, catching the apple and tossing it to Joey.

"She moved into the Dobson house," Yvonne replied. "I was walking by and saw her moving in."

Carrie, Joey, and I gasped in surprise. The apple fell out of Joey's hands and rolled away.

The Dobson house stood all by itself on the edge of Culver's Woods. The house had been empty forever.

"What a creepy old house," Carrie said. "Did you see Helga's parents?"

Yvonne shook her head. "No. It was kind of strange. I saw the moving men carrying in all this heavy, old furniture. And I saw Helga. But I didn't see any grownups."

"Weird," Carrie muttered again. Her favorite word.

I started to say something else. But I glanced up and saw Helga standing awkwardly in the lunchroom doorway. "I'm going to invite her to sit down with us," I announced, jumping up.

"Why, Maddy?" Joey asked.

"Maybe we can find out more about her," I replied. I hurried over to Helga. "I'm Maddy Simon," I told her. "I'm in your class. Want to sit with me and my friends?"

She stared back at me with her pale, gray eyes, the strangest eyes I've ever seen. *Ghost eyes*, I thought.

"No thank you," she replied. Her voice was soft and whispery. "I never eat lunch."

She's a vampire, we decided.

The four of us were always searching for vampires.

"Helga *has* to be a vampire," Carrie declared. "She never eats. She looks so old-fashioned. She keeps totally to herself. And she's as pale as death."

It was three nights later. We were crouched

across the road from the old Dobson house. Helga's house.

A long, low hedge stretched along the dark street. We hid behind the hedge, huddled together, whispering.

We couldn't help ourselves. We had to spy on her. We had to find out the truth.

The creepy old house rose up in front of us, pale in the light of the full moon. Behind the house, the trees of Culver's Woods shook and shivered in the wind.

"Where is Helga?" Yvonne whispered. "The house is totally dark."

"She's in there," I replied, my eyes on the black windows. "She's in there in the dark."

"Weird," Carrie whispered.

"I tried to talk to her in school today," Joey reported. "But she walked right past me. She wears those heavy, black shoes. But her footsteps didn't make a sound."

"Why would anyone move into this horrible old house?" Carrie asked. "It's so far from town. Nothing but woods all around."

"For privacy," I replied. "Vampires crave privacy."

The others giggled.

I thought I saw something move in the window. A gray shadow against the blackness. "Come on, guys," I whispered. "Let's take a closer look."

We crept across the road. The silence was eerie.

The only sound was the soft, steady whisper of the wind through the trees.

The old house seemed to grow darker as we approached it. We pushed through the tall weeds that blanketed the front lawn. Moving silently, we huddled beneath the big front window, pressing ourselves against the damp, moldy shingles.

"Give me a boost," I whispered to Joey. "So I can look in the window."

"Be careful, Maddy," Carrie warned. "Helga might see you."

I ignored her warning. I had to take a look. I was just so curious.

Joey and Yvonne helped lift me. I grabbed the stone windowsill with both hands and hoisted myself up just high enough to see in.

Then I stared in through the dust-smeared glass. Into a vast, dark living room. A pale square of moonlight poured into the room. I could make out a long couch, wooden and stiff looking. Two old-fashioned chairs.

I nearly toppled to the ground when I saw Helga.

"She's in there!" I whispered excitedly to my friends. "I can see her. Standing in the dark, in front of a tall mirror."

"Does she have a reflection?" Joey whispered. "Check it out, Maddy. Does she have a reflection?"

I narrowed my eyes, trying to focus on the darkness.

Vampires don't have reflections, I knew. Did

Helga have a reflection? "It's too dark to see," I told my friends.

Helga turned suddenly toward the window. She seemed to be staring right at me.

"Let me down! Quick!" I demanded. I slid to the ground.

"Did she see you?" Carrie asked, her dark eyes wide with excitement.

"I don't know," I told her. "I hope not."

"Why is she there in the dark?" Joey asked. "Did she have a reflection? Was she walking, or floating?"

Questions I couldn't answer.

"We'll come back tomorrow," I said.

The four of us met there every night. We hid behind the long hedge and spied on Helga's house. We peered into the windows. We crept around back and tried to see in through the kitchen.

Some nights we spotted a dim light in an upstairs window. Most nights, there were no lights on at all.

Some nights we saw Helga inside the house. Always alone. We never saw her parents. We never saw anyone else.

My friends and I became obsessed with Helga, with finding out the truth about her.

We tried to talk to her in school. But she stared back at us with those wintry, gray eyes and never even pretended to be friendly.

I invited her to come with us to the basketball game in the gym on Friday night. But she said she didn't like basketball.

We tried to get invited to her house. One day, Joey asked if he could come to her house and copy her history notes.

Helga said she wouldn't be home that night.

"Then how about tomorrow after school?" Joey insisted.

"It's not a good idea," Helga replied mysteriously.

She wore the same black skirt every day. She never changed her hairstyle. Her black ringlets hung down around that pale, pale face.

One day, on an impulse, I grabbed her hand. We were standing side by side in the hall at school, waiting to get into the auditorium.

I couldn't help myself. I reached out and squeezed her hand. I had to know what it felt like. I had to find out if it felt alive.

I jerked my hand back in shock when I felt how cold Helga's hand was. As cold as a winter day. As cold as . . . death.

She *is* a vampire! I decided.

She clasped her pale hands together and gazed at me with those frightening gray eyes. "It's so cold in here," she whispered. "Don't you think so, Maddy?"

It was the first time she had ever said my name, and it sent a shiver down my back.

That night, my friends and I met in front of Helga's house. Once again, pale moonlight washed over us. It was the only light except for a dim, orange glow in an upstairs window.

Crouching low behind the hedge, we stared up at the window. The shade was pulled. But we could see Helga's silhouette moving back and forth on the window shade.

"She's all alone in there," Carrie whispered. "No parents. No one."

"She's probably hundreds of years old," I whispered back.

"She doesn't look it!" Joey joked.

We giggled. But our laughter was cut short when the light in the window went off.

"She went to bed," Yvonne guessed. "Does she sleep in a coffin?"

"She must," I replied, gazing up at the dark window. Something fluttered low over the old house's sloping roof. A bat?

"All vampires sleep in coffins," Joey murmured. "Coffins filled with the ancient dirt from their graves."

"I want to see Helga's coffin," I whispered, standing up. I took a step toward the street, my eyes on the house.

"Maddy — come back," Carrie warned.

"I have to see Helga's coffin," I told her. "I have to know for sure."

We all wanted to know. That's why we spied on Helga every night.

I crept silently across the street and into Helga's front yard. Huddled closely together, the other three followed.

A twisted, gnarled old tree tilted up toward Helga's bedroom window. I grabbed a low branch and started to pull myself up.

The bark felt cold and rough against my hands. The slender branches shook as if trying to toss me off.

I clung tightly to the trunk and reached for a higher branch. Hoisting myself on to it, I peered through the leaves at the house.

Helga's bedroom window was still high above me. I glanced down and saw Carrie, Yvonne, and Joey. They had circled the tree and were peering up at me. Even in the darkness, I could see the tense expressions on their faces.

Up I climbed. Ignoring the scratch of the bark, the trembling of the branches.

Slowly, steadily, I pulled myself up. Until I was high enough to see into the bedroom window.

Holding tightly onto the trunk, I turned slowly. Lowered my head to see through a tangle of dark leaves. Gazed into the window —

— and saw Helga gazing back at me!

Her face gleamed, silvery in the wash of moonlight. Her gray eyes glowed evilly as she stared out at me, her ghostly face pressed against the windowpane.

Too startled to cry out, I started to slip. My hands slid off the trunk, and I lurched backwards.

"No!" I thrust out both hands. Grabbed the hard trunk — and held on.

"She saw me!" I called down to my friends. "Helga saw me!" I scrambled down, moving frantically, sliding and scraping down the rough trunk.

By the time I reached the ground, my three friends were already running around to the front of the house. "Wait up!" I called hoarsely.

Too late.

The front door swung open.

Helga moved quickly. Out the door. Down the front stoop. Across the weed-choked lawn to block our path.

"I know you've been spying on me!" she cried angrily. "You'd better quit it! I'm warning you!"

I stopped. Carrie, Yvonne, and Joey stopped, too. We moved together, watching Helga storm toward us.

She had her hands balled into tight fists. Her eerie eyes were narrowed at us, her face twisted in a frightening scowl.

My friends and I huddled there in the middle of the dark yard. The trees whispered and shook. The tall weeds swayed all around us.

And then the words just burst from my mouth. "Helga — are you a vampire?" I just blurted out the question, without even thinking. "Are you a vampire?"

She moved closer, her gray eyes glowing. "Yes," she whispered.

"Show us your fangs," I demanded.

A strange smile spread slowly over Helga's face. "No," she replied. "You show me *your* fangs."

I hesitated for a second. Then I lowered my fangs.

Then Carrie, Yvonne, and Joey lowered their fangs, too. Our fangs slid easily out over our lips, down to our chins.

We grinned expectantly at Helga. "Your turn," I said.

But to my surprise, Helga stumbled back and let out a frightened squeal. "I was just *joking!*" she cried. "I — I thought you were joking, too!"

"No way," I told her.

We weren't joking. We're vampires. Me, Carrie, Yvonne, and Joey — all four of us are vampires.

We were so disappointed about Helga. We had such high hopes.

But we knew what we had to do.

We formed a tight circle around her. Then we moved in.

The mystery about Helga had been solved. In a few minutes, she would be a vampire, too.

ABOUT THE AUTHOR

R.L. STINE is the author of over three dozen best-selling thrillers and mysteries for young people. Recent titles for teenagers include *I Saw You That Night!*, *Call Waiting*, *Halloween Night II*, *The Dead Girlfriend*, and *The Baby-sitter III*, all published by Scholastic. He is also the author of the *Fear Street* series.

Bob lives in New York City with his wife, Jane, and fourteen-year-old son, Matt.

GET Goosebumps
by R.L. Stine

☐ BAB47745-5	#23	Return of the Mummy	$3.25
☐ BAB47744-7	#22	Ghost Beach	$3.25
☐ BAB47743-9	#21	Go Eat Worms!	$3.25
☐ BAB47742-0	#20	The Scarecrow Walks at Midnight	$3.25
☐ BAB47741-2	#19	Deep Trouble	$3.25
☐ BAB47740-4	#18	Monster Blood II	$3.25
☐ BAB47739-0	#17	Why I'm Afraid of Bees	$2.95
☐ BAB47738-2	#16	One Day at Horrorland	$2.95
☐ BAB49450-3	#15	You Can't Scare Me	$2.95
☐ BAB49449-X	#14	The Werewolf of Fever Swamp	$2.95
☐ BAB49448-1	#13	Piano Lessons Can Be Murder	$2.95
☐ BAB49447-3	#12	Be Careful What You Wish For...	$2.95
☐ BAB49446-5	#11	The Haunted Mask	$2.95
☐ BAB49445-7	#10	The Ghost Next Door	$2.95
☐ BAB46619-4	#9	Welcome to Camp Nightmare	$2.95
☐ BAB46618-6	#8	The Girl Who Cried Monster	$2.95
☐ BAB46617-8	#7	Night of the Living Dummy	$2.95
☐ BAB45370-X	#6	Let's Get Invisible!	$2.95
☐ BAB45369-6	#5	The Curse of the Mummy's Tomb	$2.95
☐ BAB45368-8	#4	Say Cheese and Die!	$2.95
☐ BAB45367-X	#3	Monster Blood	$2.95
☐ BAB45366-1	#2	Stay Out of the Basement	$2.95
☐ BAB45365-3	#1	Welcome to Dead House	$2.95

Scare me, thrill me, mail me GOOSEBUMPS Now!
Available wherever you buy books, or use this order form.

Scholastic Inc., P.O. Box 7502, 2931 East McCarty Street, Jefferson City, MO 65102

Please send me the books I have checked above. I am enclosing $_____ (please add $2.00 to cover shipping and handling). Send check or money order — no cash or C.O.D.s please.

Name_____ Age_____

Address _____

City_____ State/Zip _____

Please allow four to six weeks for delivery. Offer good in the U.S. only. Sorry, mail orders are not available to residents of Canada. Prices subject to change.   GB394